2/17

BROKEN WING

DATE DUE

BROKEN WING

∾

DAVID BUDBILL

Illustrations by Donald Saaf

GREEN WRITERS PRESS *Brattleboro, Vermont*

Printed in the United States

10 9 8 7 6 5 4 3 2 1

Green Writers Press is a Vermont-based publisher whose
mission is to spread a message of hope and renewal
through the words and images we publish. Throughout
we will adhere to our commitment to preserving and
protecting the natural resources of the earth. To that
end, a percentage of our proceeds will be donated to
environmental activist groups. Green Writers Press
gratefully acknowledges support from individual donors,
friends, and readers to help support the environment
and our publishing initiative.

GReen
writers
press

Giving Voice to Writers & Artists Who Will Make the World a Better Place
Green Writers Press | Brattleboro, Vermont
www.greenwriterspress.com

Library of Congress Cataloging-in-Publication Data available upon request.

ISBN: 978-0-9962676-3-2

www.davidbudbill.com

All illustrations by Donald Saaf.
www.donaldsaaf.com

PRINTED ON PAPER WITH PULP THAT COMES FROM FSC-CERTIFIED FORESTS, MANAGED FORESTS
THAT GUARANTEE RESPONSIBLE ENVIRONMENTAL, SOCIAL, AND ECONOMIC PRACTICES BY
LIGHTNING SOURCE ALL WOOD PRODUCT COMPONENTS USED IN BLACK & WHITE, STANDARD
COLOR, OR SELECT COLOR PAPERBACK BOOKS, UTILIZING EITHER CREAM OR WHITE BOOKBLOCK
PAPER, THAT ARE MANUFACTURED IN THE LAVERGNE, TENNESSEE PRODUCTION CENTER ARE
SUSTAINABLE FORESTRY INITIATIVE® (SFI®) CERTIFIED SOURCING

for

Riley

CONTENTS

BROKEN WING

1.
PRELUDE

Take the road going north, further and further north. Go up through the valley, between the mountain ranges, up to where the West Running River and the River Road go west. Turn left onto the River Road, and travel through the valley. See how the mountains rise up on both sides. Then, just when you can see the little village ahead of you in the distance, slow down and turn right onto the road that comes down out of the hills to join the road that you are on. Off the pavement now, and onto the gravel road. Begin to climb up, up to the high plateau. The road gets smaller, more rutted and less used. Don't worry. Just keep going. Go straight, straight up, straight north to where the road dips down and passes through the big swamp, the one the locals call Bear Swamp, the one that spreads away wide and lonely on both sides of the road. Then climb again, up a steep slope and through the hardwood trees until you find a lane that leads off to the right, then opens into a clearing, a croft, carved out of this endless wilderness of trees. Stop your car. Park it there. Get out. Go on foot now, up the lane and up the final slope, to the dooryard, garden, orchard—for this is where The Man Who Lives Alone in the Mountains lives. Pause now. Look around. Realize how, even after all that climbing, you are still only at the bottom of an open bowl, the sides of which are mountains rising all around. Take in all you see. Then turn away. Turn toward the little house built there on the side hill, among the ancient pecker-fretted apple trees. Step up onto the porch. Approach the door. Raise your hand and knock, then wait to hear Come in! He's been waiting for you all this time. He knew you were coming. Turn the handle and step in. Take off your coat and shoes. Sit down at his table. He has bread and jam, sweetcakes, fruit and a steaming pot of tea. Help yourself to something good to eat, pour a cup of tea. Sit back now and listen to his story.

2.
SEPTEMBER AND OCTOBER

Once, a long, long time ago and far to the north, on a remote mountainside above a little village that lay far down in the valley below, there lived a man who the people in the village—and the man's neighbors on the mountain, what few neighbors he had—called The Man Who Lives Alone in the Mountains.

It is fall. Summer has come and gone. The garden lies withered by the autumn frosts. The hillsides have begun their turning from green to red and yellow. And The Man Who Lives Alone in the Mountains is busy with his getting-ready-for-the-winter chores.

He pulls up the withered garden plants and takes them to the compost heap, where they will rot back into earth so they can return again into the garden soil. Now, with all the withered plants on the compost heap, he tills the garden again and again, until the earth is clean and smooth, and there is no sign of the forest of plants that all summer he had called his vegetable garden. He has already sequestered safely underground in his root cellar or put away in his freezer or canned in jars and put on shelves the vegetables he grew in his garden during the summer.

The Man Who Lives Alone in the Mountains then turns to loading his woodshed with the wood he, last spring, cut and split and stacked neatly on the hillside beside the house under the summer sun to dry. Now he brings it into his woodshed to keep it away from the rain and the winter snows. This firewood for the wood stove inside his house will keep him warm through the darkest and the coldest time of the winter to come.

Now he takes down the screens from his windows and puts up his storm windows, and when that is done, he banks the foundation of his little house with balsam fir and red spruce boughs to keep out the cold winds, and thus he readies himself in every way for the coming winter, just as he has done every fall for all the years he has lived on this lonely mountain.

And with all these preparations done, The Man Who Lives Alone in the Mountains gets out his wintertime birdfeeders. The Man loves birds. He puts the feeders on posts and hangs them from the branches of the apple trees and nails them to the side of his house and makes himself ready to receive the multitude of feathers and wings who will soon be his companions throughout the coming lonesome months of dark and cold.

As The Man worked through his autumn chores in preparation for the winter to come, the winter itself drew nearer.

The red and sugar maple leaves that had earlier turned yellow and red had weeks ago fallen to the ground. Then the birches and the poplar, the aspen, the balm of Gilead, flared yellow momentarily and let their leaves descend to the ground. Finally, the needles of the northern larch, the tamarack, turned their own shade of yellow and also fell. Now they, along with all the other leaves, lay sodden on the forest floor. All the leaves were down except the coppery-brown leaves of the beech trees, which would cling to their branches long into the winter so they could rattle in the cold winds and then, after all the other leaves were buried under feet and months of snow, then the beech leaves would let themselves go one by one, two by two, and blow here and there, tumbling across the snow until they collected themselves in little piles, gathered together in depressions in the snow where they would remain until the next snowfall buried them, until the spring came and the snow melted and the beech leaves descended slowly toward the earth through the layers of melting snow until they met the other leaves, waiting for them since last fall on the earth below.

Then, that one day, late, late in October, after the woodshed was full, a day of unnatural warmth and sun, the day when The Man Who Lives Alone in the Mountains could see the lazy bees under the sweet and warming sun doze and feed on the chrysanthemums; this was just the kind of day The Man knew he would not see again until next May.

So, on such a beautiful day as this, he went out into the woodshed, opened the big, wide loading door, stepped inside, and took down out of the rafters his snowshoes. It seemed strange, odd, to see these tools of the deep winter leaning now against the side of the woodshed, the grass still green, the autumn sun beating down. He got himself a chair, sat down in the entrance to the woodshed, and in the warm sun, he began carefully to re-varnish his snowshoes. He applied coat after coat of varnish to the snowshoes, until the wooden frames and the rawhide webbings glistened with a soft patina that made The Man Who Lives Alone in the Mountains smile.

As he worked on his snowshoes, the fearless, friendly, curious chickadees came to see what he was doing. One particular chickadee came closer than the others. She was the one with the featherless place and the horrible scar on her breast.

Last winter, about the middle of the way through, a chickadee had started showing up at the windowsill feeder. She was distinctive from all the others because she—The Man had decided, for reasons he could not say, for it was impossible to tell, that this particular bird was female—she had a featherless, raw and torn, bloody and oozing place upon her breast, evidence certainly of some kind of attack, perhaps from an owl or a hawk or a cat, a particular cat, a cat whose name was Arnold.

About a mile down the road from where The Man lived was another house, the only one for miles around, which was where Arnold lived, with two brothers by the name of Bap, and a varying number of big dogs the Baps kept chained to posts in the dooryard, except when the two men and their dogs went bear hunting.

Because Arnold was a cat, he also just naturally liked to hunt. He especially liked to hunt little birds, and the best place for hunting little birds was in the dooryard at The Man's house. Arnold liked to saunter up to The Man's house, since the hunting was so easy up there under those apple trees among all those bird feeders. There were always dozens of birds delighting in the dooryard feast and therefore a little less on guard, less cautious, and more susceptible to Arnold's sneak attacks. Easy prey was what they were, and Arnold knew it. He preferred to attack, capture and torture his victims for as long as possible and then, more often than not, after having done what often was irreparable damage, walk away and leave his victims to their agony.

Whenever The Man saw Arnold prowling about, he hollered all manner of horrible and insulting profanities at him—and at his two owners, also—and threw sticks and stones at him and drove the cat away, but always, after a time, Arnold came back, looking for another unsuspecting bird. The Man did not keep a cat, even though almost all country people did, because he knew cats couldn't keep themselves from hunting birds.

From time to time, The Man Who Lives Alone in the Mountains entertained, if only briefly, various drastic and violent measures for being rid of Arnold permanently, but The Man, being a man of peace and serenity—most of the time, at least—never acted on these fantasies. Nonetheless, if the truth be told—as in

all stories worth telling, it must be—The Man Who Lives Alone in the Mountains wished more than anything that Arnold and the Bap Brothers and their dooryard full of dogs did not live just down the road. Oh! If only Arnold didn't live just down the road! If only the Brothers Bap didn't live just down the road!

Any wounded bird broke The Man's heart, but to suspect that it was Arnold, the cat, who had wounded this particular chickadee, who was now watching him work on his snowshoes, made The Man especially upset. Perhaps this chickadee had been wounded by a wild predator such as an owl or a hawk, but more than likely, her wound was instead the mark of Arnold's only partly feral pleasure.

The Man had named this singular chickadee Samovar, because, for some reason, the bird's little body reminded The Man of that big Russian tea urn called a samovar. The Man always seemed to come up with names for the wounded birds who appeared from time to time at his feeders. A number of years ago, there had been another chickadee with only one leg who had spent one whole winter with The Man Who Lives Alone in the Mountains. The Man had named her Peg.

Why this little, skinny, wounded bird here now reminded The Man of a huge teapot, he

could not say. Perhaps he thought to name the struggling, sickly bird Samovar because if and when the bird regained its health and stature, it would then actually be a miniature, round, whimsical version of the Russian teapot. Perhaps that is what The Man dreamed of, hoped for: the bird's body, healthy and plump, full of curiosity and song, and not the emaciated, struggling little wretch with that bloody open sore on her breast who was, that winter, every day on his windowsill.

To save the story of what happened to Samovar for some later time, suffice it to say that Samovar struggled through and survived the winter and the wound. With an abundance of the nutritious and healthful black oil sunflower seeds The Man provided every day all winter,

Samovar passed through the winter into spring and summer, then stayed on to become a faithful resident of the orchard that surrounded The Man's little house. And now that fall had come and almost passed into winter again, Samovar, exercising the usual fussy and familiar curiosity that all chickadees do, flitted over toward where The Man was sitting varnishing his snowshoes, and began to chatter the way chickadees do when they are more excited than agitated.

In The Man's imagination, he thought he could hear in Samovar's chatter the little bird saying, "What are you doing? What are you doing? What are you doing, Man Who Lives Alone in the Mountains?" The man chuckled to himself, thinking, "Boy, that's quite a mouthful for such a little bird!" Samovar ignored The Man's thoughts and continued. "What are you doing? What are you doing? What are you doing with that varnish? What are you doing with those snowshoes, those snowshoes, those snowshoes? Are you doing those snowshoes with that varnish? How do you do that? How do you do that? How do you do that, Man Who Lives Alone in the Mountains? How do you do that with those snowshoes, Man Who Lives Alone in the Mountains?"

That last day of gentle light and warming sun passed into evening, the birds went to roost, and The Man Who Lives Alone in the Mountains closed the woodshed doors with a grave sadness, for he knew what kind of change would be here in the morning. He turned to go into the house, then paused for a moment on his porch to say goodbye, farewell, and thank you to the summer and the fall, for he knew, he could feel it in his bones, that the beginning of winter stood waiting impatiently on the other side of the mountains.

And when the morning came, the cold and gray, the dank and chill of November had begun. Rapidly now, the last bit of color, the remaining pale yellows, drained away from the hillsides. Now the skeleton of the world revealed itself; the sere gray and brown of the naked hardwood trees stretched their skinny fingers against the sky. Now was the damp time, the dark time, the dank time before the coming of the snow, before the coming of the months of cold and isolation.

3.

IN THE WRONG SEASON

The feeders had been up and the birds in the dooryard for at least a couple of weeks. The usual and regular abundance of chickadees, including Samovar, were on hand to fuss and scatter sunflower seed everywhere; and, mixed among chickadees, the faithful white-breasted nuthatches and rose-breasted nuthatches. And from time to time, the flocking birds swooped down out of the sky to feed, also. Waves of pine siskins and redpolls, evening grosbeaks and pine grosbeaks, goldfinches gone brown for the winter, and purple finches all came and went daily; and, of course, there were the ubiquitous and quarrelsome blue jays.

And sometimes, in the middle of the morning, when The Man Who Lives Alone in the Mountains would suddenly hear blue jays set up a frantic clatter, he'd look out the window to see his many and varied friends, and he'd see nothing, not a bird anywhere; and when he then noticed chickadees hiding among the thick, protective branches of the balsam firs, then The Man knew to look up to the uppermost branches of the apple trees until he found a northern shrike, who had stopped by on her morning hunting run to see if she might kill a chickadee or nuthatch for her breakfast. Then, for a short time, the dooryard fell lifeless and still, until, frustrated by the emptiness and silence, the shrike flew away to better hunting grounds, and the usual busy daytime chatter and feeding of the dooryard birds resumed.

And so it was that day after day, week after week, a multitude of feathers and wings—his friendly bird neighbors—brightened the dooryard and the life of The Man Who Lives Alone in the Mountains.

It must have been about the second week of November when The Man first noticed him. Slowly, The Man began to realize that in the dooryard and at the feeders, mixed in with the chickadees and blue jays, goldfinches, pine siskins and grosbeaks, among the nuthatches and downy and hairy woodpeckers, was a common grackle.

This lone fellow, shiny and black, seemed always to be on the ground, walking and gawking around, his head bobbing back and forth as he strutted here and there. And much to The

Man's surprise and delight, Grackle held his ground in the presence of the aggressive and pushy blue jays, who were accustomed to having their way whenever they liked. But now that Grackle was here, there was at least one bird who would not be bullied by the Blue Jay Mob.

Ah, when the blue jays were not around and chickadee and pine siskin, junco and goldfinch, nuthatch and woodpecker all flitted from tree branch to feeder and back to tree branch again—all feeding, for the most part, quietly and at peace with each other, with only an occasional argument, an argument which never lasted very long and never required that the loser leave, rather only to retire for a moment, wait, and then begin, a moment later, to feed again—and, when beneath this scene of small birds in array, Grackle fed on the sunflower seeds the other birds spilled to him there on the ground underneath the feeder, it was a picture of peace and good food that any feeder-of-the-birds would love.

A picture of peace, that is, until The Blue Jay Mob arrived again and scattered all the other birds, in a panic to be away from the marauding mobsters—scattered all, that is, except Grackle. When the other birds fled, Grackle stayed and held his ground, and when the blue gang of toughs dared try to drive Grackle away, Grackle turned on them and made it clear, with an open beak, an outstretched wing and a posture threatening enough to frighten a cat, that he was not about to be driven off by the likes of these insouciant bullies. "Finally!" The Man said to himself. "Finally, somebody tough enough to put the blue jays in their place! Finally, somebody to stand up to them."

And The Man Who Lives Alone in the Mountains thought about what it had been like in this place when he had first arrived, how different he had felt from everyone else in these mountains, being as he was from away, from the city and from such a different way of life. How different and alone—threatened, even, sometimes—and frightened he had felt in this strange world.

In the early days, when The Man had first arrived here, the other people who lived scattered across this mountain, what few there were, had been standoffish and cool to the newcomer, but they in no way did anything to bother the man who meant to live alone and keep to himself on this mountain. Most of them, in fact, The Man discovered slowly, were actually quite friendly after you got to know them a little. Behind their unsmiling, nonverbal and distanced exteriors, there were some friendly, funny and very talkative people, many of whom loved to play with words, as The Man did also.

The Man discovered, much to his relief, that most of the people on the mountain were happy to leave him alone and let him live his life the way he wanted—most of the people, but not all. Not the Baps.

When The Man had first arrived in these parts many years ago, he had no neighbors. It was exactly what The Man was looking for, or so he thought. He had this whole part of the mountain to himself. It seemed like the perfect solitude. The nearest place was an abandoned farm about a mile down the road. Then, a number of years after The Man arrived, The Bap Brothers came to live on the abandoned farm—the Bap Brothers, their dooryard full of dogs and Arnold. There was nothing, of course, The Man could do about it, and they were, after all, a mile away. It was a free country, for some people at least, or so people said, though The Man knew lots of people like himself who were in no way free in this so-called free country. Yet The Bap Brothers, their hateful stares, and their hunting dogs reminded The Man too much of his childhood in the country down south, and then later in the city, also. The Bap Brothers and their ways reminded The Man too much of the place he'd spent his life trying to get away from.

There came a time, not long after the Baps moved onto the abandoned farm, when the tension between the Bap Brothers and The Man heated to the boiling point, and there was a confrontation between them in which The Man found it necessary to stand his ground and defend himself and his place, and to do so with such determination and fury that the Bap Brothers could clearly see what they were up against. After that incident, the two brothers never came near The Man again. This did not mean, however, that their resentment and dislike for The Man had abated. It only went underground.

And that left The Man with a deep sense of sadness and regret over how, so often, the circumstances that surround us are beyond our control. He had come here to be free of people who assumed they knew who he was before they knew him. He came here to be free. Yet even here, he had not found all he wanted, and the Bap Brothers seemed to stand for all The Man did not want—and furthermore, and unfortunately, they were The Man's nearest neighbors. And to make matters even worse, the Baps made no secret of how unhappy they were to have The Man as a neighbor—thus the old, ever-present worry that followed The Man wherever he went had followed him here, too.

If only the Baps and Arnold and that dooryard full of dogs didn't live just down the road!

The sight of Grackle right now, out there in the dooryard standing his ground and defending his right to be in this new place, reminded The Man of those bad, old days. Those memories began what would become a long process of an ever-deepening bond between The Man and the bird.

The next morning, here came Grackle again, walking and strutting cockily, and looking about, left and right, as he went; his head held high, full of pride and swagger. Here he came, walking down the hill from the high bog above the house, walking over the withered bracken and the sear grasses of early November, walking down the hill and into the dooryard and toward the feeder. What a handsome and self-assured figure this daring and assertive black bird made! And when the blue jays came near, Grackle opened his beak again, spread his wing, and ran as fast as he could toward the blue jays, squawking as he advanced. His posture was so threatening, so full of menace and intent, that the little black bird reminded The Man of the fierce way geese protect and defend their territory from intruders; and, of course, Grackle also reminded The Man of himself, and how he had to be sometimes, too.

What a handsome and dominant little bird this lone Grackle was! Such swagger! Such command! Yet there was nothing bullying about Grackle. He never ran other birds off in order to eat himself, but rather simply sidled in among the others, be they siskins, tree sparrows or red polls, and began quietly to eat the sunflowers the other birds spilled down to him.

All the ground-feeding birds were much smaller than Grackle, and it would have been easy for Grackle to run them off, but he never did. All it seemed he wanted to do was join them. All it seemed he wanted was what they all wanted, also: just something to eat. "Just like me," The Man said softly to himself. Yet when he had to, as when the blue jay toughs arrived, Grackle was able to drive them away and put them in their place. "Just like me," The Man said softly to himself.

Surely, Grackle would be king of the dooryard feeders and apple trees from now on, and a just and fair-minded king, as well. A shiny, iridescent, beautiful, black king. "Yes. That would be good," The Man said softly as he smiled and nodded to himself. "Yes. Just like me."

And a comical king he was, too. When Grackle ate, it was a sight to see. The nuthatches and chickadees picked a seed from the feeder and flitted to a branch, where they held the seed between their tiny feet and with their beaks, banged open the shell, and then picked out the inner meat. The pine and evening grosbeaks rummaged around on the platform feeders, picked up an un-cracked seed, and with an amazing feat of beak dexterity, they rolled the seed around in their seed-cracking bills until the shell fell away, after which they ground down the meat a little in their large and mighty beaks—which is why they are called *gros*-beaks—and then down the gullet it went. But Grackle, comical King Grackle, gawked and bobbed across the lawn until he found a seed, then tilted his head back, and with exaggerated, odd and laughable jerks of his head and neck, and with his beak wide open as if he were trying to gulp down something much too large, he swallowed the seed, apparently whole, then went on to another seed, where he went through his ridiculous and amusing routine all over again.

After a few days of waking each morning to find Grackle there again and feeding, The Man began to realize that he'd been watching Grackle unawares every day for a couple of weeks, at least—or so it seemed—since the end of October. That wasn't right. Grackles left sometime toward the middle of October, along with all the other late-leaving summer birds. Why, then, was this one still here?

The next day, The Man Who Lives Alone in the Mountains waited with his binoculars for Grackle's return. Through his binoculars, he could see clearly what without the binoculars he could only vaguely see. As Grackle moved across the lawn, The Man could see that Grackle's right wing protruded awkwardly from Grackle's side, and a number of primary feathers jutted off the wing at an unnatural angle. Through the binoculars, he could see that Grackle's entire right wing did not fold properly against Grackle's body. On Grackle's left side, his good wing folded neatly and smoothly against his body— it disappeared as birds' wings do when folded and not in flight—but on his right side, his wing stuck out roughly, the feathers protruding jaggedly away from Grackle's body.

There had been some kind of accident or attack, and the reason Grackle was still here with the winter birds was because he had not been able to leave with the rest of his kind. Grackle couldn't fly.

He had been left behind. What could have happened? How could Grackle have been wounded in this way? Hawk, bobcat, coyote: all possibilities, The Man thought to himself. Possible, but not very likely; he had a pretty good idea how this had happened.

What was it like for Grackle to be stranded

in this northern place? Did he have any idea what the northern winters were like? Was he afraid? What was it like to be the only one of your kind left in a place, stranded, abandoned, alone among so many others so unlike yourself? How lonely must he feel?

The Man knew how he had answered these questions for himself, years ago when he had first come to this mountainside. But now, here with this single grackle, it was different from The Man's arrival. When The Man had come to this place, it was by choice; he had come here because he wanted to, wanted to be away from where he had been. The Man had come here because he loved the mountains and the birds in the mountains, and he loved gardening and growing apples. He loved the wilderness. He wanted to be a farmer, just as his ancestors had been, and his parents, as well. So his arrival here was not by accident, not something fate had visited upon him, as it had this hapless grackle in the dooryard now.

Not a day went by that The Man Who Lives Alone in the Mountains didn't think about, didn't remember, his old life in the city, didn't remember the life of the street, of meeting and visiting with friends on the corner, of sitting in restaurants or in the park and laughing with friends. Nor had he forgotten what the night was like in the city, so full of life and noise and music, music, music, so unlike the country down south where he had grown up, or this northern wilderness where he now lived. He hadn't forgotten any of that old life, the life he had abandoned. And when he remembered it, he felt sad and restless with his present life, and he often longed to return to his old life, his life in the city, return to his own people; yet he never did. He never did. Not even for a visit. Never.

And all of these memories, these recollections, made bright and clear for The Man how Grackle must feel now, to be the only one of his kind left in a place, stranded, abandoned, among so many others so unlike himself. And these memories of The Man's old life, his recollections of the way he used to live, created in The Man a deep feeling for the life and plight of this little black bird, who now walked and gawked around the dooryard.

As the days passed, The Man watched his friend, who he had now named Broken Wing. The Man watched Broken Wing more and more intently, and, as is always the case, the more closely you watch, the more you see, and the more you see, the more you begin to understand, and the more you understand, the deeper and stronger your feelings become for that which you are watching and seeing and coming to understand.

And his increasing understanding made The Man wonder how he could have been so mistaken about what he had been watching earlier. Clearly, Broken Wing was neither tough nor self-confident, neither cocky nor self-assured. Instead, Broken Wing was desperate, frightened, alone. Broken Wing was in danger of starving to death. The Man got more and more involved in Broken Wing's crippled life, and what was surely his impending and imminent death.

He got out his bird books and began studying the habits of the common grackle. As he looked at the pictures and read about the bird, he knew something was wrong. He took the books to the window and looked at the pictures of the grackles in the books, then he looked at Broken Wing. Broken Wing's tail was too short, his whole body too small to be a grackle; and his feathers, though somewhat shiny, did not have, especially around his head, the purple-blue iridescence grackles have. And Broken Wing's beak was more curved than a grackle's beak. Slowly, it became obvious to The Man that Broken Wing was not a grackle.

The Man began studying other blackbirds. Finally, there it was: a picture and description of Broken Wing.

Size and shape of a red-winged blackbird or robin, but with a slightly longer tail. Sometimes suggests a short-tailed grackle, but lacks any iridescence to feathers in the fall, when general appearance is rust-brown. Bill is more slender at base and more curved at tip than other blackbirds. Eye is yellowish-whitish and feathers are rusty only in October.

A rusty blackbird. Broken Wing was a rusty blackbird, which explained why The Man saw Broken Wing descend out of the high bog behind the house each morning.

The bird book also said:

Habitat: Wooded swamps and damp woods with pools during migration; boreal bogs in the breeding season.

Above The Man's house was a high bog, a quaking bog, full of sphagnum moss and hummocks growing stunted spruce and fir trees; here and there, the rare, insect-eating pitcher plant; and on the edges of the bog, two different kinds of lady's slippers, the orchid of the north.

Behavior: a secretive and solitary bird . . .

The Man smiled to himself. "Just like me," he said.

. . . the rusty blackbird is most often seen during migration, when small parties may be found walking about on the floor of wet woods, turning over dead leaves in search of insects. They seldom occur in very large flocks, and do not, as a rule, associate with red-winged blackbirds or grackles.

The Man had never seen a rusty blackbird—this solitary fellow who does not, as a rule, associate with other blackbirds—before in his life; yet here he was now, stranded here in the wrong season, abandoned to his own devices, trapped in the north country, where he and his kind were meant only to live for the spring and summer, raise families, and flee south again before the cold and dark northern winter turned their soft, spongy boreal swamps into frozen and inhospitable places fit only for the snowshoe hare, the ruffed grouse, the moose and deer who lived in such a place year-round.

The Man Who Lives Alone in the Mountains marveled at the idea that for all the years he'd lived in this place, rusty blackbirds had been arriving every spring to nest in the high bog just above his house, breed and raise their young, and then leave in the fall, only to return again in the spring, every year, year after year, for more years than he had lived here. For hundreds of years, for thousands of years, rusty blackbird families had been making homes and young in the bog above his house. It made The Man feel shy and humble, as if he were only a visitor here, someone just passing through, here only for a short time and then gone, perhaps himself gone back "home" to the city, back to his own people, whereas the rusty blackbirds really belonged to this place, and had belonged to this place for a thousand years.

Well, on the other hand, The Man was here, too. He'd nested here, too: cleared land, built a house, pruned the ancient apple trees, made a garden. He was a part of this place, too, even if he was the newest of the newcomers. No need for him to feel too out of place or too shy. No, there was no need for him to apologize for his presence here. Besides, as he chuckled and said to himself, "I'm a kind of rusty blackbird myself, in habitat and habit. The only big difference is, I don't have feathers or wings—but I'm a secretive and solitary bird, that's for sure!"

So, a new neighbor. No, an old neighbor. No matter—neighbors nonetheless.

The Man Who Lives Alone in the Mountains thought about the meaning of the word neighbor. Ever since The Man had been a little boy growing up in the country, and then as an adult living in the city, he'd been interested in words. *Neighbor*: one who dwells nearby. The word came from two other words: *nigh*, meaning near, not far off, close; and *boor* or *Boer*, not from the English language but from the Dutch, meaning a peasant tiller of the soil. Therefore, a tiller of the soil, a farmer who lives nearby: *nigh-Boer*. Neighbor.

The Man raised vegetables and apples, and took care of and harvested his woodlot. He was a farmer. Broken Wing lived with his family in the bog above the house, and he and his family spent their days turning over dead leaves and probing around in sphagnum moss, looking for insects. They lived near each other, and therefore they most certainly were *nigh-Boers*, neighbors. What a pleasant thought to think of these rusty blackbirds as his neighbors. And what a different thought from thinking about the Bap Brothers as his neighbors!

Insects! Suddenly, as if a little explosion had gone off inside his brain, The Man shouted, "Insects! Insects! How could I have been so stupid?" He banged himself on his forehead with an open palm. "Jumping to conclusions again, before you really know," he said to himself. "I've been the victim of people doing that to me my whole life, and here I am now doing it myself!"

Once again, The Man shook his head incredulously as he realized how wrong he had been about his interpretation of what he had seen. As he had learned earlier, Broken Wing was neither cocky nor self-confident; he was, instead, struggling to survive. Now, The Man realized also that Broken Wing was not being comical when he went through his antics to get those unshelled sunflower seeds past his beak, down his throat and into his crop, where hopefully they could be ground into something he could then digest, and from which he might get some nourishment. He was desperate.

Broken Wing was a rusty blackbird, an insect-eating bird. His beak was a probing, snapping beak, a slender and curved beak made for finding and catching insects. It was not a short, compact, seed-crushing beak like the grosbeaks and redpolls have, and not even like the slightly more delicate chickadee beak, or even the pointed nuthatch beak, which was adapted to both seeds and insects. Broken Wing's entire beak, head, throat and body were built to find and catch insects. Insects! His attempts at choking down those sunflower seeds were not some kind of comedy, but the motions of desperation. He was eating those unshelled sunflower seeds because he was starving to death, and there was nothing else for him to eat.

The Man got his boots out from behind the wood stove and put them on. He threw on a coat, grabbed a light pair of gloves out of the glove box in the mudroom, picked his car keys from the nail on the mudroom wall and headed out the door, across the yard and toward the car. He got in the car, started it, roared down the lane, and turned left onto the road that traversed the high plateau. Down the road he went, down the mountain to the valley below. When he reached the highway, he turned left again and drove east along West Running River Road—back the way you came to get into this story.

He drove east to the town next to his town, a bigger town than his little village, the town where you turned left onto the West Running River Road, a town with a feed store in it. He pulled into the feed store parking lot, got out of his car and went into the store. He bought twenty-five pounds of a mixture of cracked corn, cracked wheat and millet, and headed home. Surely, one of these milled and smaller seeds would be easier for Broken Wing to get down his throat.

When he got back home, he poured a little pile of the mixed seeds on one corner of the platform feeder, scattered some of the grains on the ground in various places, then went inside and waited. It wasn't long until Broken Wing reappeared. At first, he went to the sunflower seeds and began choking them down, as he had done before. Then—and how it happened, The Man didn't observe—but suddenly, he saw Broken Wing pecking at the crushed and milled seed scattered on the ground, and he noticed that Broken Wing didn't tilt his head back as much anymore, nor did he make those ridiculous straining motions with his head and neck

to get the seeds down his throat. Now, he kept his head down most of the time and foraged among the seeds on the ground, continuously pecking, pecking, pecking, pecking, pecking, pecking, filling up his crop with this new food which was so much easier for him to eat.

The Man realized that not only was Broken Wing stranded, abandoned in this northern place, the only one of his kind among so many strangers—and not only did he know nothing about winter—he was also alone in this unfriendly place, without any of his kind of food to eat, for all the insects he liked best were dead.

As happens every year, as fall comes on, whole species of insects lay their eggs in the ground, in the cracks and hollows of trees, wrap them up in a chrysalis woven onto the branches, burrow them into a weed stem and make a gall, and then all the living members of that race die and trust the future of their species to those eggs buried and hidden until the winter passes and spring comes again.

Except for the occasional hatch of cluster flies or ladybugs or some other insect on a warm November or later winter day, Broken Wing would be without his favorite food during the entire winter to come. The crushed, milled grains of corn and wheat and millet would have to do until spring, which meant that Broken Wing was dependent on The Man for his life. Without The Man's help, Broken Wing would surely die.

Every day, The Man woke up and began his day long before the sun came up, especially now that the dark time of the year had come and the sun was slow to rise and quick to set. He rose long before the sun and long, long before the birds. The birds preferred to wait until daylight had washed away the last traces of the night before they pulled their heads from under their wings and emerged from their roosting places in the deep softwoods on the leeward side of a hill somewhere—where, even when the wind blew the hardest, it hardly penetrated into the dense center of the softwood trees. For Broken Wing, there were plenty of protected, dense and quiet places in the bog above the house where he could roost each night.

In the summer, it was different. In the summer, the birds were awake and singing, often before the dawn. In the summer, by the time daylight came, the air was filled with their cheering, joyful song; but now, in the winter, no bird sang his or her summer song, no bird came awake and began to feed before daylight was certainly upon the earth. In the dark time, there was only time to eat and sleep and try to stay warm, only time to survive, to hang on, until the spring.

One morning, a few days after The Man Who Lives Alone in the Mountains first put out the new, crushed, milled seeds for Broken Wing to eat, after The Man had been up for awhile and after the birds had arrived at the feeders, The Man glanced out the window and saw Broken Wing on top of one of the platform feeders, a feeder which was nothing but a board nailed to a post and a post sunk into the ground. The post and platform were about five feet off the ground, and The Man wondered how Broken Wing had gotten up there. Had he jumped? Could he—could any bird—jump that high? If he couldn't fly, how did he get up there?

A few days later, as the birds fed in and among and under the apple trees in the dooryard, the blue jays suddenly set up a terrible squawking, and all the birds instantly flew away and hid in the protective branches of the nearby balsam fir trees. This sounding of the alarm from the blue jays usually meant that there was a predator near; and sure enough, as The Man scanned the sky, he saw a hawk circling above the yard. It was not a shrike, but a larger hawk of some kind, and a late-migrating one—for usually, by this time in November, the hawks had also gone south for the winter.

Broken Wing! Save Broken Wing! The Man scanned the ground under the apple trees to find his wounded friend, but he was nowhere to be found. Then, there he was, up in an apple tree, safely hidden beneath the tracery of branches that separated Broken Wing from the hawk above. There was no way the hawk could maneuver through that complication of branches and get to Broken Wing, and when the hawk realized that, she tilted her body sideways and soared, banking away on her steady wings into the invisible distance.

But how did Broken Wing get onto the platform feeder? How did he get up into the apple tree?

Later that day, as The Man watched the birds out his window, the birds startled again and flew away; and much to The Man's surprise, he saw Broken Wing flutter awkwardly up into the apple tree. He could fly— poorly, ineptly, but he could fly! Just enough to get himself up into a tree and out of harm's way. And what was even more amazing, he flew with only one wing. This time, The Man saw Broken Wing actually jump into the air, and then, beating his good wing frantically, rise up until he got himself into the apple tree. There was nothing very pretty or graceful about how Broken Wing flew, but he flew nonetheless.

Every day now, as November slid toward December, the days got shorter, the nights longer, and both the days and the nights got colder. Winter was coming; yet The Man felt cheered and hopeful. Having found something Broken Wing could eat and having discovered that he could actually fly, if only just a little, there seemed a chance, just a chance, that Broken Wing might make it. With The Man Who Lives Alone in the Mountains helping, Broken Wing might make it.

4.
INTO THE CENTER
OF WINTER

The days passed uneventfully. Thanksgiving approached, arrived, and left. Then it was December and getting colder, and the thermometer dipped down into the single numbers, dangerously close to zero, almost every night. The Man Who Lives Alone in the Mountains knew that birds must eat huge amounts of food daily just to stay alive, and now, in cold weather, they needed even more. And as if that weren't difficulty enough, Broken Wing, being a migratory bird, couldn't add an additional layer of downy feathers close to his body just for the winter, as the chickadees and blue jays and other northern birds did. Broken Wing would have to make it through the cold without his favorite food, without a down jacket for the winter, and, worst of all, with only one wing. The Man knew that it was going to be hard, maybe impossible, for Broken Wing to survive, and he wondered if Broken Wing, down deep in his instincts somewhere, knew that, too.

But, in spite of all the dangers and difficulties, as the days progressed deeper and deeper into the center of winter, Broken Wing actually seemed to improve. Perhaps it was the nourishment he was getting from the cracked corn, wheat and millet, or perhaps only the healing that time can bring. Whatever it was, The Man couldn't say, but Broken Wing most definitely seemed to be improving. He was a permanent fixture now among the birds at the dooryard feeders; he seemed at home and comfortable, less skittish and on the lookout all the time. The little birds, and the blue jays too, were now used to Broken Wing; he'd become a regular in this wintertime community of feathers and wings. And often, now, The Man would see Broken Wing hop into the air, flap a few flaps with his good wing, and make his way up to the platform feeder or up into the apple tree.

The Man began to realize that although Broken Wing was slowly regaining his ability to fly, like all rusty blackbirds, Broken Wing was a bird who preferred to walk or run, like the ring-necked pheasants and bobwhite quail who lived in the country where The Man, as a boy, had grown up. Both the pheasants and the quail were strong flyers, yet they preferred to stay on the ground and walk or run to where they wanted to go; they flew only when they absolutely had to, to escape danger—or, in the rusty black-bird's case, to migrate. Well, that was fine on bare ground, and with two good wings—but here in the north, and now, as December wore on, with it snowing more and more every day, the snow piling up deeper and deeper with every storm—here and now, what would Broken Wing do? How would he get through all that snow?

And so, just when things seemed to be improving for Broken Wing, along came another difficulty, this ever-deepening snow, to make his life that much harder. And this particular December was unusually bad, for it snowed almost every day, and the snow was dry and fluffy, making it even harder to get through. Yet each morning, about the same time every day, The Man would see Broken Wing come fluttering and thrashing through the new snow, his one good wing flapping out to one side like an outrigger on a canoe, there to stabilize himself as he plowed, flapped, swam, and flew through that fluffy, light and airy white sea, down out of the bog above the house, down the hill, down toward the door-yard and the feeders.

The Man thought about the time, a long time ago in the city where he came from, when he had seen a legless man on a low, little cart, pushing himself down the sidewalk with his hands. He thought about the young boy he'd seen, not long ago, with a withered leg and foot—who, with the aid of his crutches, dragged his useless leg and foot along. Both the man and the boy, like Broken Wing, went determinedly about the days of their lives, crippled as they were, yet nonetheless coping, going on, dealing, making it from day to day. He thought about the legless man in the city from long ago, and the boy he'd seen just recently. As he looked out the window at Broken Wing, The Man was full of admiration and respect for these three cripples, and for their tenacity, courage and perseverance.

Then, as sometimes happened with The Man, a little explosion went off inside his brain, and again he banged himself on his forehead with an open palm. He had gotten an idea how he could help Broken Wing—how he might make Broken Wing's life a little easier.

That afternoon after lunch, The Man went into the woodshed, took down the snowshoes that were hanging on the wall, and went out into the snow. He put the snowshoes on, strapping his boots into the snowshoe harnesses and tightening them down well so they would not come off as he tromped through the deep, soft snow.

The Man went back and forth under the dooryard apple trees, packing down the snow. Then he started up the hill behind the house, up into the woods and high bog, following Broken Wing's fluttering, thrashing trail in the snow, up to where he knew Broken Wing stayed at night. Carefully, he made a trail up into the bog and back down to the house again. He packed the snow down into a smooth, broad roadway so that it would be easier for Broken Wing to get down from the bog to the house, the apple trees and feeders.

The next morning, The Man watched intently so as not to miss seeing Broken Wing amble down the smooth, broad path he had made for the wounded bird. He waited. And waited and waited. And waited.

Then, finally, from a direction Broken Wing had never approached from before, here he came thrashing and flapping through the loose and deep unpacked snow, ignoring the broad, smooth, packed path The Man had made.

First, The Man was baffled. Then he was hurt. Then one of those little explosions went off in his brain again, and he said out loud, to himself, "How could I be so stupid?" As he was wont to do, he banged his forehead with his open palm.

What The Man had done in his effort to be helpful and kind had made Broken Wing's life even more difficult. He had put Broken Wing more in harm's way than ever before. All that those nicely-packed trails had done was to announce to every predator around exactly where Broken Wing went each night—and not only that, the nicely packed, firm trail gave the predators a convenient road to travel on to hunt down and kill the wounded bird The Man most wanted to protect.

This incident got The Man to thinking about his urge to be helpful. The Man realized that he had begun to interfere too much in Broken Wing's life, and that he needed to think harder about what being helpful really meant and about how he might back away from sticking his nose, and his snowshoes, too far into Broken Wing's business, which was his independent, private, and personal struggle to survive.

That afternoon, The Man went out on his snowshoes and packed some false trails, trails that led away from the bog in the woods above the house where Broken Wing lived, trails that led to nowhere but a deep snowdrift off in the wrong direction, trails that would deceive would-be predators and lead them away from

Broken Wing. The Man tried to undo the harm he'd done.

As he headed home that afternoon, The Man spoke out loud to himself. He often talked to himself, as many people do who live their lives alone. "On the other hand, never jumping in to help isn't right, either."

And The Man began thinking about his birdcage in the house. It was a thing of beauty, four feet high, tall and spacious and wide, made of bamboo, and empty. The Man kept no domestic household birds, but had the cage for a temporary residence, a kind of bird hospital, for those birds who, on occasion, might fly into a window of his house.

On certain days, when the quality of light was just right—or, better said, dangerously wrong—on certain days when the glass in the windows of the house reflected the trees in front of them so perfectly that they became deceptive, treacherous, and sometimes deadly mirrors, the birds flitting about the house became confused when looking in the direction of the windows, for they could not see the window, but rather, only more woods and trees. Even though the woods and trees they saw were false, reflected woods and trees, these birds, on occasion, flew into the woods that were not there, crashing headlong and full-speed into the window glass.

Sometimes, sadly, they were killed outright, their necks broken by the impact; but most often, they'd hit the window obliquely or at a slow enough speed so they were only stunned, knocked unconscious momentarily. It was at these times, when The Man heard a bird hit the window, that he would rush outside, pick up the bird, and, cradling it gently in his hands, bring it into the house. He had discovered over the years that if he stood by the wood stove and let the warmth of his hands and the heat from the stove work its way into the body of the unconscious bird, that the bird would revive more quickly than if it were left outside in the cold and wind. Besides, here in the house, the bird was safe from predators who were always on the lookout for an opportunity to take a meal with little effort, such as an unconscious bird upon the snow.

After a time of cupping the wounded bird in his hands and standing next to the warming stove, the bird would begin to revive. The Man could see this by the way in which the bird would open its eyes and begin to blink; and then, after a little more time, begin to move its head from side to side. It was at this moment that the man would take the bird to the beautiful and empty bamboo birdcage, open the door, and set the still-woozy bird inside on a perch.

The Man referred to the beautiful bamboo cage as the Recovery Room, which is what it was, for after a time—the length of which varied with each bird and the extent of its injury—of the bird sitting, dozing and nodding on the perch, slowly, the wild bird would revive, look around, and realize to its terror that it was in a cage. The bird would begin to fly madly at the sides of the helpful and beautiful cage which was, of course, from the bird's perspective, an ugly and evil enclosure. It was then that The Man would leave off whatever he had turned his hand to and come to the frantic bird, open the cage door, reach in, capture the bird in his hands, and take it out to the porch where, after a few kind words of admonition, caution and farewell, he would release the winged creature.

As The Man and his snowshoes headed for the house that afternoon, he again spoke out loud to himself: "This is tricky business. How to help, yet not get in the way. Now, that's not so easy."

Just then, he thought he saw a cat print in the snow on the old trail that led up the hill and into the woods, toward the bog where Broken Wing spent the night. He paused, knelt down, and examined the track. Yes. A cat print for sure, a small one, the print of a housecat, not a bobcat or a lynx, and, no doubt, the print of the cat The Man hated most: the Bap Brothers' cat, Arnold.

Danger, The Man understood clearly, was always all around.

And so it was that afternoon that The Man Who Lives Alone in the Mountains learned to back off a little, become less involved in Broken Wing's struggle to survive; yet he began also to realize how complex and difficult it was to understand what "helping out" really meant. More and more, he stood attentively and watchfully to one side, but remained prepared and ready to do what he could for his wounded friend.

The next morning, The Man sat down at his desk to write a letter. The Man liked to write letters, especially these days. He liked to write letters to an old friend with whom he had just recently been back in touch after many years of silence, an old friend who still lived in the city from which The Man had come those many years ago.

Dear Howard,

A little intro to what I want to tell you: Yesterday afternoon I noticed that the barometer was unusually high, and had been that way all day. I knew we were in for an early cold snap. I guessed it would probably get down well below zero. This is not unusual in January or early February around here, but it doesn't very often happen here in the middle of December. I figured it would be an excellent night to defrost my freezer.

As night fell and the temperature did, too, soon it was colder on the porch than it was inside the freezer, where it was only zero, so I emptied out the freezer and put the contents out on the porch. When I had the freezer defrosted, I brought the frozen food in from the porch and I was all done before I went to bed.

In the process of cleaning and rearranging the frozen food, I came upon numerous things I wanted to throw away: partial loaves of bread, freezer-burned old hamburger and hot-dog buns from so long ago I couldn't remember when, some chunks of ancient, dehydrated, unidentifiable cheese, and so on. I had a washtub-full before I was done.

I took the discards out to the garden. It was a cloudless night. It's always cloudless on a night as cold as last night.

I threw these freezer discards onto the garden, where I throw all my kitchen scraps and other compostable materials all winter long. Often, deer come out of the softwood trees into the garden under the cover of overcast darkness, or under the full moon and across the glittering snow to eat what's there. What they don't eat rots back into soil in the spring.

Before I begin my story, I've also got to tell you that the ravens around here live high up in the highest trees, on the highest peaks in the mountains to the east of where I am. Even though my place is about two thousand feet off the valley floor five miles down the road from here, I'm still only at the bottom of an open bowl, the sides of which are mountains rising all around. And in those mountains, to the east of here, is where the ravens live.

Now. To my story. You may not believe what I am about to tell you, but I want to tell it to you anyway.

This morning, as I drank my tea and watched out the window toward the garden where I'd thrown the freezer scraps, I saw a most amazing and inspiring sight.

Two ravens appeared, circling above the garden. Lower and lower over the garden they descended, circling, circling, coming in for a landing. Then—bump, bump—down onto the snow.

These birds are huge. They are so much bigger than crows, and they have big and not-at-all-crow-like beaks. And they have shoulders—actual shoulders, or they at least look like shoulders—like a person's, not a crow's, or like other smaller birds—but more like an eagle's.

The two ravens began immediately to walk around, taking their big, humorous, gawking steps, looking the situation over, their heads and shoulders bobbing

back and forth. They walked to and fro, inspecting the new additions to the scraps lying on the snow. Then they set to work, and in less than an hour, these two ravens had hauled off to their secret aeries in the mountains to the east everything I had dumped out there.

They worked, they hauled, they went back and forth, attending to nothing but their chore. They ate nothing during this time; they worked and hauled and did not rest. And they worked cooperatively, even though they were taking what they took in different directions, or so it seemed. One rose and went through the draw below the garden and banked to the right and off toward the mountains to the east. The other rose and flew down through the draw below the garden and banked to the left and off toward the mountains to the east. Were they going to different places? To different secret stashes? Different hideouts? Or were they both headed for the same place from two different directions?

At first, they came and went together, both arriving and leaving at the same time. While they were both there together in the garden, sorting through the various kinds of breads, these two ravens never once quarreled with each other. Blue jays or grosbeaks in this situation would spend more time arguing with each other over who got what than they'd spend getting it.

At first, the pieces were so large they couldn't fly off with them. You know how hamburger buns come four or six all baked together in one piece, so that you have to pull them apart. They couldn't haul off that many, that big a single piece all at once, so they set to reducing them to a manageable size, which they did by pecking and banging at them and breaking apart the hamburger and hot-dog buns until they were a size appropriate for hauling away, something they could get up into the air with and fly away.

And their flight pattern for takeoff was always in the same direction, always the same way of leaving: they took off into the wind, and their return was in the same direction each time, also. They'd come in, circle a few times, lower with each circle, their legs and feet out, exactly like an airplane's landing gear, and then—bump, bump—they were down on the snow, and back to sorting through the breads.

I tell you, we had an airport here this morning. Slowly, their flight schedules separated, so that they were coming and going at different times. Occasionally, one raven got stacked up above the other, and had to circle for a moment while the other landed before he could make his final approach.

And then, when they had hauled off all the larger pieces, they set upon the smaller pieces, one slice of bread at a time—but right away, after the first take-off with one of those single slices, they knew it was too light a load, and they circled back and dropped down again, knowing that a trip of the distance they were making was not worth it for only a single slice of bread. For a short while, each bird picked up a single piece of bread, then put it down, then picked up another, as if they were looking for those now-gone, heavier, larger pieces. For a moment, they paused, as if confused or thinking. Then I saw something I have never seen before and don't think I'll ever see again.

The two birds, each of them—I saw this, as I was watching them through binoculars—began to put one slice of bread on top of another, and another on top of those two, and so forth until they had made a stack of three or more slices, which they then, with some considerable effort, got their beaks around and flew off with. They had figured out that if they stacked the slices up, they could fly off with more than one slice at a time!

This hauling out loaded and coming back empty went on until the job was done. When it started, there was a considerable pile of bread out there, and when they were done, there was no bread whatsoever visible in the snow.

With their work done, both birds came back and ate something—maybe the cheese, maybe scraps of bread, it was impossible to see exactly what—but they ate as if, with the job done, they could now relax, have a beer, eat some dinner and hang out for a little while. They ate some, and visited some, right there in the garden; then they rose up one more time, this time together, and together flew away.

Howard, who could be luckier than I am? How could I be so fortunate? To live in this place with neighbors such as these, to be in their lives and they in mine, to make a community between us, to share this place with them—what could be better than that?

And this afternoon, when I snow-shoe out through the woods off toward the eastern mountains, will two of the ravens who invariably come croaking over to see what I am doing, to see what's going on, will two of them be the bread delivery guys? How could I be so blessed to be alive in such a place?

I think that's it for now, except to say I'll write to you again sometime soon, and tell you about this wounded rusty blackbird who has been hanging around here all winter. I call him Broken Wing. It's quite a story. But that is for another time. For now, I hope that you are well and staying warm.

Your friend,

5.
THIS TIME TO WATCH
AND WONDER

The Man's attentive and concerned involvement with Broken Wing continued throughout December and into the darkest and coldest time of the winter, while at the same time, he learned to step back, distance himself, from the little bird's struggle to survive.

While it was indeed the darkest and the coldest time, the center of winter, it was also, to The Man Who Lives Alone in the Mountains, the brightest and best time of the year. The snowbanks along the sides of the road grew higher and higher, and the mercury in the thermometer dropped lower and lower—some nights down to 25 or 35 or even 40 degrees below zero—and on those nights, the blue-black dome of heaven revealed a myriad of constellations, across which flowed that dense river of stars people call the Milky Way. And if the sky was that clear at night, then usually the days, even though they were short, were brilliant, also. Light flooded through the windows of his little house and filled The Man's days with an intense clarity. Oh, how The Man loved these days of deep snow, sharp, stinging cold, brilliant blue skies and blinding white light.

The intense cold and deep snow isolated The Man and his bird friends from the outside world. This made The Man happy, not fearful or sad. The woodshed had ample wood for the wood stove; he could stay warm through the coldest time, and there was plenty of food for both himself and his feathered friends. The Man felt as though he and his bird friends were cut off from the rest of the world, hidden in a secret place far toward the interior of a strange land of cold and snow, and these notions made The Man happy. The insularity and solitude that these winter days brought filled The Man with an odd and quiet joy, and because of the isolation and remove of these deep winter days, The Man knew a kind of relaxation during this time that he knew at no other time of the year. He enjoyed himself and the short days, the long nights, and the world around him with a renewed, intensified, and quiet pleasure.

The sameness of these days, the cycling of light and dark, blended as the days passed one into the other, following each other seamlessly except for an occasional storm that came to add another foot of snow to the already snowy landscape. In the sameness of these days, The Man found not only pleasure, but greater focus and an intense passion, as well; for now, he could attend to his inner thoughts and to the endless turning of day into night—in other words, both his inner and the outer weather—and, of course, to the birds he loved so much, who kept him company just outside his windows.

In this time of pensive reflection, this time to watch and wonder, full of stillness and light, The Man Who Lives Alone in the Mountains one day sat down to write another letter.

Dear Howard,

That time of darkness and light, cold and emptiness is here. I want to tell you about what happened yesterday. Another bird story.

I got up before sunrise—which isn't very hard this time of year, since the sun doesn't come up around here until well after 7:30—and went about my morning chores. I started a fire in the stove, put the water on to boil, went to the bathroom and peed, brushed my nappy hair, washed my face, and brushed my teeth. Details! Details are important! When the water boiled, I made a pot of tea.

Sometimes, on an especially cold winter morning, I like to get back into bed with my tea and not stand at the window. While the fire warms the house, I drink my hot tea under the warm covers, and I watch out the back window to a different birdfeeder and wait for the dawn.

When dawn came yesterday, or just before the dawn, when the morning light had begun to overcome the darkness, a single chickadee appeared at the feeder and began her breakfast. In less than ten seconds, a dozen of her brothers and sisters and cousins were at the feeder, also.

This morning, as I watched the little birds, I wondered at the way they always seem to arrive together in a group, or very nearly. I know chickadees don't sleep together, but rather roost, each to him or herself. How, then, did they all get to the feeders at just about the same time? Is someone the leader? Does she wake up the others? Does she sing a few notes? Do they "sense" the dawn while their heads are still tucked in the warmth and absolute dark of the down beneath a wing? Do they all get hungry at exactly the same time? How do they all know to get up and come to breakfast together? Are they simply social creatures who enjoy each other's company, and would never think of eating breakfast alone? And where does that social, collective impulse, this ability to act and be together, come from? These questions got me to wondering about other kinds of birds.

Lately, in the afternoons, there has been a large flock of redpolls—in other winters, it might be a flock of pine siskins—sometimes as many as fifty, pecking and scratching across the surface of the snow beneath the feeders, finding whatever it is they find in the husks and hulls and refuse from the feeders above. They look, for all the world, like a flock of tiny chickens as they hunt and peck and bob—but then, so un-chicken-like, suddenly—away they all go, all together in perfect unison, up into a nearby tree.

Sometimes, this upward flight has an obvious cause, like a threat from an approaching shrike or the yap of a dog; but often, there is no apparent cause for this flawless, unified and simultaneous rising up together. How does that happen? How do they do that?

I've often seen the same thing driving down a wintertime dirt road, as snow buntings who have been pecking along the surface of the road gathering sand and gravel for their gizzards get up and blow away in a swirl, as if they were a little bunch of dry leaves caught in a dust devil.

Much larger birds do this, also—like the wintertime flocks of evening grosbeaks who visit the dooryard feeders and who can, it seems at will, display this perfect-unison takeoff from the branches of an apple tree. And in the spring, large flocks of blackbirds, starlings and grackles and red-winged blackbirds, literally fill up the naked branches of a poplar tree—hundreds of birds together in one flock—and then, suddenly and simultaneously, all lift off and exit at exactly the same time, as if all these birds were really one bird with many wings.

And, in a way, more amazing is the same phenomenon among fish. Many times I've seen huge schools of fish, sometimes thousands of individuals in one school, moving together this way and that, up and down and away, waving back and forth like a fan, like a relaxed hand, in the water; again, as if these thousands of fish were a single individual.

In all of these examples, the group moves together, simultaneously, without a leader—or so it seems.

How do they do that? Is it that they have some kind of collective mind or soul that lives outside each individual body? And if this mind-soul does live outside, away from, each individual, if it lives in the space between the individuals of the group as a whole—whether it is a flock of birds or a school of fish—and if this is the consciousness of no particular individual, but rather the consciousness of all, of the group—if all of that, then: are these individuals not really individuals, but only parts of a larger individual? Are they only the arms and legs and fingers, fins and wings of a bigger individual called the flock or the school?

Can it be that the mind-soul of this larger individual really does exist in the empty space among and between the members of the flock, yet controls the entire flock from that empty space?

And how can these birds be individuals one minute, sitting on a shelf feeder, pecking open a single sunflower seed and arguing, fighting with each other; and in the next moment, lose, or give up, their individuality to the group, to that larger mind-soul, that bigger individual called the flock? How can they do that?

Could I, could you, give up my, your, own individual self to a larger flock of humans, and if you or I did that, what would that be like? I'm not sure about you, but I am, I fear, too much the solitary individual to ever be able to do such a thing.

What I'm talking about is why I'm so attached to Broken Wing, my rusty blackbird friend. As my bird book says: a *secretive and solitary bird—they seldom occur in very large flocks, and do not, as a rule, associate with red-winged blackbirds or grackles*. We are two of a kind, he and I. Both of us cast adrift on this white and foreign sea. And, well, as you know, birds of a feather flock together, even if only to remain apart. Another loner, like me. Which the problem. He and I are loners, and yet we're both also more than that.

Each bird is an individual first, and a member of a flock second, just as you and I are. Yet some individuals are more inclined to be members of flocks, like grackles; or like you, Howard, living there surrounded by others of your, and our, kind, while some individuals, like Broken Wing and I, for whatever reasons cause us to be that way, are more solitary and less inclined to be members of a group or flock.

Yet now that I say that, I know that although it's true, it's also not true. You and I both know full well that each and every single bird or fish does not give up its individuality to the group, at least not all the time. Rather, I think what they do and how they move so perfectly in unison together is not by abandoning their individuality, but rather by some kind of higher form of communication within this group of individuals. And this higher form of communication is something most, almost all, human beings never experience.

But you and I, Howard, have experienced it. I know you already know what I'm talking about. I'm talking about when we used to play music together, you and I and our friends.

I think birds in flocks are like we used to be, when we played together, how we could jump into a tune and play it—without any discussion before we began of what we were going to do—because we all could communicate so well with each other on our instruments, we all understood each other so well musically, that there was no need to talk.

And once we really took off and entered that other world—call it the Tone World, which is what William calls it—once we were in the Tone World, there really was some kind of collective personality that took over, that made us one being, a flock of four or five, like the birds and the fish; and we, I'm sure, appeared to those listening to us to be a single, new and different person, a single instrument playing—which, of course, is exactly what we were.

And yet none of us ever gave up playing our own individual instruments or playing out of our own personal and individual lives, and because of that, each of us played our own individual instruments out of some deep place in our own personal and individual selves. We were, each one of us, absolutely different from the other, yet all of us, while we were playing together, made together a single song. We made a new and different person while we played together. We were, at those moments, just like the birds and the fishes, don't you think?

It's not that flocks of birds or schools of fish or groups of improvising musicians are, when they are together, a single living thing with a collective personality, or that they are always only separate individuals who are just great at communicating with each other as they play together; it's that they are both of those things and both at once. At least, we were at those times when we really did leave this everyday world and pass over into the Tone World.

The thought of being my individual self within the group, yet also joining the group, becoming part of that larger mind-soul, that bigger individual called the group, the flock, the band, and thereby knowing a kind of higher communication between individual souls, the thought of all of that, the thought of being there with you and the others, of sharing life and music with all of you: all of that sounds so good to me!

Oh, Howard, I'm so homesick! Thinking about all this makes me so lonesome for you and for the others, for the street, for all those people, all those sounds, the noise, the music of the city, our neighborhood. I'm homesick for those times we played together. I want to do something, make something, create something with a group, with our group, and not always, as I do here, alone. Alone. Alone. I'm not meant to be alone.

Well . . . I read a poem the other day by a Chinese poet named Hê Chih-chang called "Coming Home," which, by the way, was written more than a thousand years ago::

I left home young. I return old,
Speaking as then, but with hair grown thin;
My people meet me, but they don't know me.

They smile and say:
"Stranger, where did you come from?"

You see? What if I did come home? Who would know me? What good would it do? No. This exile is my home now.

I know you and a lot of others back there think I was out of my mind to come here all those years ago, way up here to this cold, white world. And staying here all these years has just proved to all of you that you were right! But I couldn't help it. I had to come here. I had to leave there, I had to leave home. I couldn't stand it there anymore. When I came here, I was just trying to be who I am, and not who somebody else says I am, and that's what I'm still trying to be.

Do you know that great quote from Thelonious Monk? "A man is a genius just for looking like himself." Well, it takes a lot of courage and work to look like yourself, "simple" as that may be. And Howard, sometimes the sacrifices I have to make to look like myself are almost more than I can stand.

I know another poet—I can't remember his name right now—who got it right when he wrote:

When I was young I dreamed of home
And in my dream
I saw a place remote and in the mountains.

Now I'm in that place
And I call it home,

Yet home is still nowhere I can find.

It must be nowhere
Is the right place,
And when I get there I'll be home.

And until I get to nowhere, I'll be here.

And yet, so much of the time
I am so sad and blue.
So much of the time I am so lonely,
Sad and blue.
And sometimes, sometimes I just
Don't know what I am going to do.

Your friend,

The Man finished the letter, put it in its envelope, sealed it, addressed it, and put on his outdoor clothes, and as he walked down the lane to the road and the mailbox, his eyes welled up with tears.

He opened the mailbox door, put the letter in, closed the door, put up the flag, turned, and headed back up the lane and toward the empty, silent house.

6.

TROUBLE ON TOP
OF TROUBLE

That night, it snowed about six inches. The next afternoon, as The Man walked back up the lane from the mailbox with the mail, he could see the story of many animal lives printed in the new snow.

Here, two red squirrels had dashed back and forth through the snow, going who knows where, doing who knows what, but both going and doing whatever it was with the derisive jeers and snickers and spasmodic jerks of feet and tail with which red squirrels do everything.

And here, a partridge had walked calmly and in a straight line through the snow, obviously going somewhere, its feathery feet holding itself up remarkably well; as did the webbed feet of the snowshoe hare, whose tracks wandered about up and down the lane and over the snowbanks on either side. And over here, a few hare pellets, droppings, scattered about as if waiting there to be periods at the end of sentences.

And there: the track of a cat, a housecat: almost without a doubt, the hated Arnold.

Then, as The Man moved further up the lane toward the house, he gave up studying the snow and looked up momentarily, just in time to see something he thought he'd never see.

There, right before his eyes, came Broken Wing: gliding, fluttering, flying down the hill from the dooryard apple trees toward the large white spruce that stood alone in the field below the lane. Yes, Broken Wing—gliding and flapping, not just with one wing, but two! Gliding and flying, actually flying, haltingly and awkwardly, but flying nonetheless, the couple hundred feet from the dooryard apple trees to the white spruce. It was clear that the effort took everything Broken Wing had, but he was doing it. He was actually flying, and with both wings. The Man stood amazed and full of hope at what he saw.

As Broken Wing landed safely on the tip of a spruce branch and began to walk toward the middle of the dense and protective tree, The Man turned and headed up the hill toward the house, shaking his head and wondering at what tenacity, perseverance, struggle and dogged will can do.

The days at the center of the winter passed almost seamlessly now, one into the other, yet within their steady pace and sameness. Slowly and daily, the light lasted longer at both ends of the day.

Day and night and day again and night, the cycle of the days moved slowly on.

The Man loved the regularity and sameness of these days, and he knew, in spite of his constant isolation and loneliness, that he could never live happily without them.

It was certainly true that much—well, some—of the time, he lived unhappily in this place, but trying to imagine living without this place and days like these was an equally unhappy thought. "Damned if I do and damned if I don't," he said to himself as he moved up the hill and toward the evening.

Another morning, and The Man was in his kitchen again, dropping a little milk into his cup and pouring the tea on top of it until his cup was full. He stirred the tea, stood at the kitchen counter, drank his tea, and looked out the window, out beyond the apple trees and toward the garden.

As The Man stood at his kitchen window drinking tea and watching the birds at the feeders, he thought he saw, out of the corner of his eye, a dark and vaguely familiar shape

scurry behind a snowbank beyond the door-yard apple trees. Nothing. The Man must have been mistaken, yet he continued to watch that place where he thought he had seen a strange, yet almost familiar shape; thought he saw some movement, but nothing, only the birds feeding at the feeders or on the ground or at rest in the trees. Nothing, nothing but the stillness and the calm of another clear-cold winter morning.

Then, suddenly exploding out of the snow-bank and upward into the morning air, all fur and fang and claw, The Man saw Arnold leaping toward the lowest branch of the nearest apple tree, where now he could also see Broken Wing resting, his back turned to the danger about to overwhelm him.

"No! No! No! No, you son-of-a-bitch! You bastard! No!" The Man screamed as he ran without coat or boots out the door, down off the porch and into the snow.

As soon as The Man appeared on the porch screaming, Arnold left off his attack and turned, and was now running down the lane toward the road below the house as fast as he could go. The Man leapt the few dozen yards to the apple tree, his now-wet stocking feet burning, to where Broken Wing lay fluttering, flapping in the new snow, trying to stay on the surface of this white and airy sea where just now he was literally drowning in the frothy, frozen water.

And where he beat his wings, the snow was red with blood. Although Arnold's attack had been thwarted, the wing that Broken Wing had been painstakingly mending all last fall and this winter was now torn and broken again.

As The Man stood over Broken Wing, the helpless bird beat his wings weakly in the bloody snow. The Man could not leave him here. To do so would be to invite certain death, if not from a passing, or perhaps right-now-watching, predator, then from suffocation, drowning in the snow; and if not from that, then from the bitter cold. As much as The Man wanted not to interfere in the life of his little friend, The Man knew he must act and act quickly, or there would be no life left in which not to interfere.

The Man bent down and lifted the blood-soaked bird carefully and gently out of the snow. Now, on top of the trauma of the attack and the danger of the snow and cold, Broken Wing had also to deal with the fright he felt at being in the hands of, for all he could tell, a creature more dangerous than a cat. So frightened, in fact, was Broken Wing that he became still—what appeared to be calm. He was, however, anything but calm; rather, he was in a state of something

closer to a coma, such was his agony and terror in this moment.

The Man labored through the deep snow toward the porch, his stocking feet still burning from the intense cold. Gingerly, he carried Broken Wing into the house. He stood for a moment next to the wood stove, thawing out and warming up his frozen feet and hoping that the warmth might also revive Broken Wing a little, also. But Broken Wing did not respond. He lay bleeding, cupped in The Man's hands, his eyes wide open and blinking, but his body absolutely still. Broken Wing, it seemed, was frightened nearly to death, yet fully alert and prepared for whatever fate awaited him. The Man looked down at Broken Wing and marveled once again, as he had so many times since last October, at this small and brave life that lay now bleeding in his hands.

He moved to the counter in the kitchen, elbowed away the cutting board, the bread and butter and jam and teapot that had been his breakfast, and laid the bleeding and terrified bird down on the counter. The Man un-cupped his hands. Broken Wing didn't move. The man ran some water in the sink, adjusting the temperature to something just a little warmer than lukewarm. Still, Broken Wing did not move. The Man washed his bloody hands, then wetted a cloth and began to daub at the blood, now already solidifying into clots on Broken Wing's black feathers. He cleaned the broken wing as best he could and dried it carefully, patting at the wet feathers with a soft, dry towel. All this time, Broken Wing lay absolutely still, his eyes still wide open and staring at The Man.

As The Man worked on Broken Wing's wing, he realized that of course, this was not the first time Broken Wing and Arnold had met. Arnold was almost surely the cause of Broken Wing's original injury early last fall, and Arnold was also, no doubt, responsible for the scarred breast of Samovar, the little chickadee.

When The Man had washed and dried Broken Wing's broken wing as best he could, he wrapped the bird in a clean, dry towel, and moved back to the wood stove again, where he stood for a long time, letting what he hoped was the heat and comfort of the warm stove and the clean towel salve Broken Wing's terror. If Broken Wing was, in fact, comforted by The Man's efforts, he showed no sign of gratitude— only that wide-eyed, blinking resignation in the face of what was surely, still, to Broken Wing, the terror of his impending death.

The Man moved across the room to the beautiful, four-story, bamboo birdcage. He held Broken Wing in one hand, opened the door to the cage with the other, and put the bird inside the cage, hoping that he would be able to grab onto a perch and sit there upright and not fall over. Broken Wing did just as The Man had hoped. The Man closed the door, stepped back, and watched his caged, wild friend. Broken Wing did not look at The Man anymore, but looked straight ahead with that same wide-eyed, blinking stare. Then Broken Wing closed his eyes and appeared to fall asleep.

For a time, The Man watched Broken Wing; then, when he was somewhat assured that Broken Wing was truly asleep, or at least resting comfortably, The Man turned to his morning's work.

Some time passed, The Man didn't know how long; though it must have been quite a while, because The Man had sunk deeply into his work when he heard a thrashing and banging in the birdcage. When he rose from his desk and came to the cage, he saw Broken Wing on the floor of the cage, striking out at the walls with his one good wing. The Man knew it was far too soon to let Broken Wing go, too soon to release him into the out-of-doors. What was he to do? Perhaps if he put a blanket over the cage, made it dark, he could convince Broken Wing it was night, and the bird might go to sleep—or at least get quiet, and thus help himself recover.

He drew a tiny cup of water from the faucet and placed it on the bottom of the cage. He poured a small amount of the cracked corn, wheat and millet mixture on the floor of the cage. Then he went to one of the windows in the living room and captured about a dozen ladybugs in a small jar who had hatched out that morning and were crawling around now on the window glass, and put the jar of ladybugs in the cage, also. Then he covered the cage over with a blanket, and after a time, during which there was some sound under the blanket—The Man hoped it might be Broken Wing having himself some seeds and water and ladybugs—all got quiet.

The rest of the day passed, and there was nothing but silence from the cage beneath the blanket. Darkness came. The Man made and ate his supper, then sat in the evening beside the warming wood stove, picked up a book, and opened it at random to a poem by Mêng Hao-jan:

RETURNING AT NIGHT TO LU-MEN
MOUNTAIN

A bell in the mountain-temple sounds the
coming of night.
I hear people at the fishing-town stumble
aboard the ferry
While others follow the sand-bank to their
homes along the river
... I also take a boat and am bound for Lu-mên
Mountain—
And soon the Lu-mên moonlight is piercing
misty trees.
I have come, before I know it, upon an ancient
hermitage,
The thatch door, the piney path, the solitude,
the quiet,
Where a hermit lives and moves, never
needing a companion.

When he was finished reading, The Man realized he had been so distracted by what was or was not happening under that blanket over the birdcage that he hadn't heard, in his mind's ear, a single word of the poem. He got up and moved across the room. After all, it had been hours, all day, since he'd gotten Broken Wing to settle down by putting the blanket over the cage. The Man went to the cage and lifted the blanket.

There he was, Broken Wing, alive and looking around; and this time, when he saw the light from the room and the face of The Man, Broken Wing began again to beat wildly at the walls of his cage. Quickly, The Man dropped the blanket again over the cage and put Broken Wing back in the dark. Slowly, Broken Wing got quiet again. The Man prepared for and went to bed.

In the morning when he awoke, and after he'd started a fire in the wood stove and put the water on for tea, The Man went to the birdcage and lifted the blanket. As soon as Broken Wing saw the daylight, he began banging again with his good wing on the bars of the cage. The Man knew he must let Broken Wing go. Even if he wasn't as healed as he ought to be, he had to let him go. He could not keep this wild bird in the dark for days. To let him see the light was to release his wild and desperate desire to be free.

Outside, it was not safe. Dangerous Arnold was out there somewhere waiting, as were hawks, bobcats, fishers, and the punishing weather; but all those dangers, The Man knew, were better than the safety of this cage. Broken Wing was crippled, handicapped, lost in this white sea of the north country, the only one of his race left in these parts now; but all those handicaps notwithstanding, The Man knew it was better to be in danger and free than to be safe and in prison.

He went to the mudroom and put on his heavy boots, toque and winter coat, then he returned to the living room, opened the cage and reached in. He took Broken Wing again in his cupped hands and went out onto the porch, pausing there for a few moments so Broken Wing could accustom himself to the cold winter air and the brilliant white light of another crystal, blue-clear morning. The Man stepped down off the porch and into the snow and went to the nearest apple tree, reached up and placed Broken Wing on a branch, and went back into the house.

He watched Broken Wing now from the kitchen window, watched him do nothing but sit there in the winter morning. The Man watched and watched and watched until his patience ran out and he turned to his work.

Broken Wing had work to do, too. He had to begin all over again, as he had months ago, begin to try to heal his broken wing so that he might again have a chance to survive; and now, again, he had to do it all on his own.

When, after a time, The Man looked up from his work at the desk and turned his gaze out the window to that particular branch on that particular apple tree, Broken Wing was gone. The Man smiled to himself. In his smile was both pleasure and fear: pleasure at what seemed like Broken Wing's boundless and indomitable will to survive, and fear for the wounded bird's perilous future.

The Man Who Lives Alone in the Mountains went to his bookcase and took down from the shelf a book—the title of which was *The Complete Poems of Paul Laurence Dunbar*. The Man opened the back of the book, went to the index, and scanned down through it until he came to "S," and then to "Sympathy." He opened the book to page 102, and read:

SYMPATHY

I know what the caged bird feels, alas!
When the sun is bright on the upland slopes
When the wind stirs soft through the springing grass
And the river flows like a stream of glass;
When the first bird sings and the first bud opens,

And the faint perfume from its chalice steals—
I know what the caged bird feels!

I know why the caged bird beats his wing
Till its blood is red on the cruel bars;
For he must fly back to his perch and cling
When he fain would be on the bough a-swing;
And a pain still throbs in the old, old scars
And they pulse again with a keener sting—
I know why he beats his wing!

I know why the caged bird sings, ah me,
When his wing is bruised and his bosom sore,
When he beats his bars and would be free;
It is not a carol of joy or glee,
But a prayer that he sends from his heart's deep core,
But a plea, that upward to Heaven he flings—
I know why the caged bird sings.

"Yes," thought The Man Who Lives Alone in the Mountains, "Yes, I too know how a pain still throbs in the old, old scars, and yes, I also know why the caged bird beats his wing. Yes. Yes. I know why the caged bird sings."

Beginning that day, The Man kept an especial eye out for the hated Arnold. And much to his surprise and delight, he realized now that it seemed the quarrelsome blue jays were also standing guard as they never had before; for now, whenever Arnold approached the door-yard, the blue jays set up a terrible racket, a squawking holler, the likes of which they usually saved for a marauding hawk or owl.

Quietly and to himself, The Man apologized to the blue jays for all the nasty thoughts he had harbored toward them over the years—well, maybe not all the nasty thoughts. The Blue Jay Boys were still the pushiest, most obnoxious denizens of the apple orchard. Yet The Man could see now, in spite of their noisy, quarrelsome and overbearing nature, that they, too, were an important and welcome part of this dooryard community of many birds and one man. They were the watch-birds of the bird yard.

In fact, one morning about a week after The Man had released Broken Wing, he saw Arnold coming up the driveway, but before he could put some clothes on and run outside to drive the cat away, he saw a squadron of blue jays take off from an apple tree and attack Arnold the way small birds do to crows who are out to steal eggs, or the way crows attack an owl. The blue jay squadron yelled and screamed and hollered and dive-bombed Arnold into a dither of confusion, and sent the hapless cat running down the road.

The following weeks passed uneventfully, and Broken Wing seemed to recover from his latest insult and injury faster than he had last fall. In just a couple of weeks, it seemed he was almost flying again.

The end of winter was upon the land, and the first faint hints of spring hovered at the corners of the days. In the late afternoon, the light lasted longer in the southern sky. In the morning in the east, "the rosy-fingered dawn" brought with it now the promise of something different, something to do with warmth and life. The house eaves dripped. Down cellar, potatoes began to sprout, onions collapsed, winter squashes molded and fell in upon themselves.

7.
THE STORM

The next day dawned partly cloudy and still. As The Man Who Lives Alone in the Mountains moved about his early-morning living room, he noticed that the barometer—which he reset every night before going to bed—had fallen dangerously low. Then, as he drank his tea and looked out the window, he noticed that there were more birds in the dooryard than there usually were at this time of the morning, and all of the birds were feeding more actively than usual. They all moved from feeder to branch and back to feeder again quickly, almost frantically. The barometer, the unusual activity of the birds, and "that feeling in his bones" all told The Man that a storm was coming.

All morning, the clouds thickened in the north and west, as if someone were laying out blankets on the surface the sky—gray blankets, each blanket a shade grayer than the last—until by early afternoon, the sky had the steel-gray coloration that everyone in these parts knew meant serious snow.

By noon, the barometer had fallen even lower. Around two o'clock, in the stillness, the calm that so often precedes a storm, it began very gently to snow. Light flakes floated down leisurely through the still air, so peaceful, so quiet. By three o'clock, the snow fell more thickly; by four, the wind began to blow. All The Man could think about was Broken Wing. Where was he? Would he make it through this storm? What could The Man do to help his wounded friend?

Then he remembered that at about noon, he thought he'd seen Broken Wing glide his awkward cock-winged flight from one of the dooryard apple trees down across the lane and into the big white spruce tree in the little field below the house, something Broken Wing was doing regularly now that his reinjured wing was once again beginning to heal. The least The Man could do, he thought, was take some seeds in a little cup and put them down under the spruce tree.

The Man dressed for the out-of-doors, went into the woodshed and scooped a few handfuls of cracked corn, millet, and other seeds out of the garbage can where he kept them, and put them in a small container. He headed down the dooryard hill toward the spruce tree.

It was snowing hard now, and blowing, too; and the west wind blew the wet snow into The Man so hard that it hurt his face and stuck to his clothes. The wind was blowing so hard it almost knocked The Man over. When he reached the spruce tree, he got down on his hands and knees and crawled under its broad and arching branches toward the trunk. Here, at the base of the large tree with its branches bowing low under the weight of the snow, only a little of the wind and snow could enter. It would be a good place for a wild animal to ride out this storm. The Man hoped that Broken Wing was hiding safely somewhere in this tree.

"Broken Wing!" The Man shouted over the noise of the storm, "Here are some seeds! In this little cup here. Here are some seeds! I'll put them down here at the base of the trunk. Here's some seeds!"

It never occurred to The Man Who Lives Alone in the Mountains to think of himself as ridiculous as he crawled on his hands and knees under a white spruce tree out in the middle of a blizzard on a lonely mountainside, hollering over the noise of the storm to a wild bird. It never occurred to him to think such thoughts, because there was no one else around to have to worry about. Right now, at least, for The Man, there was only The Man Who Lives Alone in the Mountains and Broken Wing and a multitude of other non-human creatures, moving about vaguely, almost unseen, in the background of his life.

Suddenly, and much to The Man's surprise, just above him, less than an arm's length away, there was Broken Wing. "Oh, Broken Wing! I'm so glad you're here. Here's some seeds. I'll put them here on the ground at the base of the trunk."

The Man started to back away on all fours, then stopped. His mind raced. "Maybe the best thing for me to do is try to capture Broken Wing and take him into the house for the night, just for tonight, just one night. That way, he'd be safe. Maybe he wants me to save him. Didn't he, after all, come down from wherever he was to see me? Didn't he come to my call? He knows me. He knows I want to help him. Dare I reach for him?"

The Man reached for Broken Wing and Broken Wing hopped away, just far enough so The Man could not get to him. Then Broken Wing waited, his eyes focused steadily on The Man.

"No, I should never have reached for him. I should leave him alone. He doesn't need me.

No. He does need me. He'll surely not survive without me. I've got to try to capture him. It's for his own good."

The Man reached again for the wounded bird, and again Broken Wing hopped away, again just far enough to be out of reach. "Broken Wing! It's me! Your friend. Come into the house with me, just for tonight. Please! Come in."

Once more, The Man reached out for Broken Wing, and once more, the bird withdrew. The Man sat down on his haunches and dropped his chin into his chest. Then, The Man Who Lives Alone in the Mountains raised his head and looked directly at Broken Wing.

Farewell, my friend. Godspeed.
I pray that you may pass this night
safe within the branches of this tree.
I also pray, and earnestly, that when
morning dawns upon our world,
we shall see each other once again.
Take care. Be safe. My friend.

And with that, The Man Who Lives Alone in the Mountains crawled backwards out from under the branches of the white spruce tree and struggled through the ever-intensifying storm, up the hill toward his house.

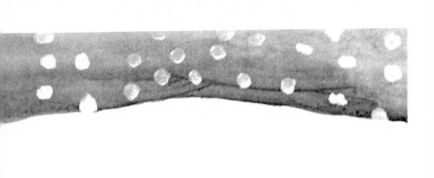

The storm raged more fiercely now. The wind howled down the road toward his house like a freight train barreling down the track. The wind blew so hard it took his breath away. He had to cup his hands around his mouth and nose to break the wind just so he could breathe. He slogged and staggered up the little hill to his house and porch, then through the door, and he was safely home.

He took off his coat, hat, and mittens, and shook the snow from them. He took off his boots. He stood at the window then, and looked out through the blowing and drifting snow, through the last bit of the day's light, toward where the white spruce tree now appeared for only one more brief moment as a shadow, a vague apparition, a ghostly figure tossing and bending before the force of the storm. Then it was dark, and The Man turned from the window, lit the lamps, and began preparations for his supper.

The wind blew even harder. The house swayed on its foundation, as if it were a boat cast upon a stormy sea. It shook as if some wrathful beast had grabbed hold of the house with its huge hands. There was nothing for The Man to do but wait for the storm to pass. He remembered a poem from long ago. He went to his bookshelves and took down a book called *The Complete Poems of Ralph Waldo Emerson*. He opened it, and read:

THE SNOWSTORM

Announced by all the trumpets of the sky,
Arrives the snow, and, driving o'er the fields,
Seems nowhere to alight: the whited air
Hides hills and woods, the river and the heaven,
And veils the farm-house at the garden's end.
The sled and traveler stopped, the courier's feet
Delayed, all friends shut out, the housemates sit
Around the radiant fireplace, enclosed
In a tumultuous privacy of storm.

"Well," he said to himself, "This farmhouse certainly is 'veiled,' as is 'the garden's end,' but there are no 'housemates' here."

Nor was there a fireplace. Rather, a large cast iron stove, up next to which The Man now stood listening to the wind howl outside, wrapped as he was in "the tumultuous privacy of storm" with a book in his hand.

"'Tumultuous privacy of storm,' indeed," he said to himself again as he put the book down, took a log out of the wood box, put it in the cast iron stove, and moved to the kitchen to begin work on his supper.

What Emerson's poems left out, and what The Man knew all too well, even from the privacy and security of his house, was the terror of the storm to those who must be out in it: those like Broken Wing. Emerson's view was an observer's and an observing view, distanced, removed, and therefore able to see the beauty in something which, at closer range, was frightening.

There was another stanza to the poem, one that described the aftermath of the snowstorm. The Man thought it best to read that one after the storm had passed.

For now, however, the storm continued to rage, sometimes slackening in intensity just long enough for The Man to begin to think it might be coming to an end; yet always, it seemed only long enough to gain more strength and resume again stronger than before, as if the lull had been only some kind of respite in which the elements had gathered even greater strength for yet another, more intense assault on all that clung now so perilously to the earth.

Supper done, The Man tried to distract himself with a little reading. Reading wouldn't do. There was nothing left but to hope and pray.

The Man went to bed. As he lay in his bed listening to the storm's furious wail, he wondered about Broken Wing, wondered if he'd eaten any of the seeds out of the little cup, wondered whether he was still safe within the embracing branches of the white spruce tree. The Man Who Lives Alone in the Mountains wondered if he'd ever see his friend again.

The blizzard raged on into the night, at the center of which The Man and his house and the world around him, including the white spruce tree below the lane and its inhabitant, now lurched and trembled toward an uncertain dawn.

8.

INTERLUDE

The Man pulled up the covers, turned out the bedside light, turned on his side, and fell asleep. And in his sleep, he dreamed. It was a pleasant dream that night, in spite of—or perhaps because of—the peril all about him.

Like the white spruce tree below the road, where, hopefully, Broken Wing still hid, The Man's little house stood strong against the storm that night, just flexible enough to bend before the punishing winds, yet rooted in its place deeply enough also to hold on.

In the morning, when The Man awoke, the storm had passed. The day broke clear and bright and calm, as if the terrors of the night had never visited that place. Yet one look out the window gave evidence of the storm's passing and effect. A new landscape shone bright under the morning sun. The Man went to the book of Emerson's poems he'd left on the table last night, and now read the other stanza of "The Snow-Storm."

So fanciful, so savage, nought cares he
For number or proportion. Mockingly,
On coop or kennel he hangs Parian wreaths;
A swan-like form invests the hidden thorn;
Fills up the farmer's lane from wall to wall,
Maugre the farmer's sighs; and at the gate
A tapering turret overtops the work.
And when his hours are numbered, and the world
Is all his own, retiring, as he were not,
Leaves, when the sun appears, astonished Art
To mimic in slow structures, stone by stone,
Built in an age, the mad wind's night-work,
The frolic architecture of the snow.

From the safe perspective of the quiet and warm house, the results of the snowstorm did, in fact, look "frolic," but The Man knew that for those who had to ride out that storm, as if in an open boat cast adrift upon a cold and angry sea, there was nothing "frolic" about what had happened overnight; rather, "savage" was the word.

This had been the kind of storm that is devastating to the plants and animals and trees who must survive unprotected. Again, The

Man thought to himself, "Another lesson in how appearances deceive, since what appears so whimsical and beautiful, so 'frolic,' is, in fact, a picture of pain and destruction as dangerous as Arnold's fangs and claws."

This beauty now that he saw out the window was as deceiving as an ice storm that puts a glaze on the world so that in the morning, after the storm, when the sun rises into a clear sky and shines on the ice-encased and glittering landscape, one might forget for a moment that this picture, too, deceives. Under that beauty lies a similar destructiveness, for the weight of the ice breaks off whole limbs of trees, or bends younger trees down into permanently deformed shapes.

Again and yet again, the world around The Man delivered lesson after lesson in how appearances—and ignorance of what lies behind those appearances—distort and deceive. Just the way, The Man thought to himself, people look at me and see what they want to see instead of who I really am.

The Man got dressed for the out-of-doors. He had to push hard against the door, against the two feet of snow piled against it, to move the door even a little bit. When he had opened it enough to squeeze out, he worked his way to the woodshed door, opened it, and stepped into the snowless woodshed, where he found his shovel. As he went about digging out from the storm—there must have been somewhere between two and three feet of new snow—his attention and worry turned increasingly to Broken Wing.

He dug new paths to the dooryard feeders, cleaned them off, and filled them up. With his tractor, he plowed the lane, filled in during the night from bank to bank—*fills up the farmer's lane from wall to wall*—with snowdrifts four and five feet deep, down to the road. Then the Man came inside, made a cup of tea, and ate his breakfast.

Slowly, the birds descended from the softwood thickets above the house and returned to the feeders. First the chickadees, then the nuthatches, then the downy and hairy woodpeckers, then a flock of evening grosbeaks swooped in, announcing with showy aplomb that they, too, had made it through the night. All morning, The Man watched for a medium-sized rusty blackbird.

Then, about noon, seemingly out of nowhere, there he was—walking around on the new snow beneath a feeder, eating seeds. "Broken Wing! Broken Wing! Welcome back, my friend!"

As often is the case in the north country, the biggest storm of the winter is also the last.

Quickly, now, beginning the very day after the storm, the sun seemed to rise higher and shine brighter and warmer.

And the constant snows turned to rain, rain glaze on snow, and then mud and ice and snow. Yes. Spring, struggling to arrive.

Light hovers now longer in the southern sky. Brooks uncover themselves. Alders redden. Evening grosbeaks' beaks turn green. Chickadee finds the song she lost last November, and the Blue Jay Mob abandons argument and gluttony; they crane their necks, they bob their heads, they bounce on the naked branches of the apple trees and cry: Spring!

"What?" The Man says, "What? Could I have heard a phoebe?" Yes! There also, on a naked branch of an apple tree, flicking her tail downward, calling her insistent, maddening call, over and over again. Yes. Phoebe.

Now, The Man Who Lives Alone in the Mountains walks out upon the earth, walks through the warming air, under the strengthening sun, ankle-deep in mud.

He turns his attention to his feathered summertime friends and moves across his little piece of mountainside, cleaning and repairing the many birdhouses he has scattered throughout the orchard and along the side-hill where he lives.

And when all the birdhouses are ready for their summer inhabitants, The Man moves over to a scattered bunch of old tires, restacks them, six or eight of them, to make a tower about four feet high. He levels the tires carefully, then takes the garbage can lid that lay next to the tires, and carefully places it upside-down on top of the tires. Then he fills the garbage can lid with water and—voilà!—a birdbath and a drinking station for his summer friends.

Wind and rain. A rush of wings. Spring. The trees loud again with birds.

There, in the balsam fir, a golden-crowned kinglet searches for a mate, a place to build a nest. Flocks of shy, slate-colored juncos scurry, flit across the dooryard lawn, foraging through the husks of seeds, saying again, this year, only *Tick. Tick. Tick. Tick. Tick. Tick.* Red-winged blackbirds and grackles—their heads and necks a springtime opaline; savannah sparrow, fox sparrow, tree sparrow, chipping sparrow, song sparrow, and white-throated sparrow, silent still.

Brown-headed cowbird, house finch, purple finch, goldfinch, robin. Killdeer in the open fields. Power lines dotted with sparrow hawks, kestrel. And at night, The Man can hear, down below him in the open fields, the woodcock whistle and snout.

Birch and popple catkins droop. Popple and red maple push out new leaves. The geese return; their long V's plow the fields of cloud. High and far away, they seem strange, mysterious as the new leaves.

Below them, the chickadee, like a friendly hand, remains: close, diminutive, minimal, half-forgotten in the yet-still-bare dooryard apple tree.

And here. The myrtle warbler dressed for spring. Bright white, blue bright, gray and yellow light…who doesn't warble at all, but cheeps and says, *this is sour, acid soil, is spruce and fir, is north, is where I make my nest.*

And in the evening, the veeries warble and sing their liquid descending glissando, dreaming they are falling water, as they have done in this place year after year for a thousand-thousand years.

Then, one midday as The Man works about his place, he catches out of the corner of his eye just a glimpse of a large bird as it comes down quickly, falling, plummeting down out of the sky. It swoops, tilting on strong wings through the hardwood trees at the edge of the meadow, disappearing into the deep woods. Even that slight glance is enough for The Man to know that the red-tailed hawk—the big hawk with the little voice—who nests high up in the yellow birch that hangs out over the ravine and waterfall just beyond the garden, where the deep woods begin—has come again this year to lay and hatch her eggs and raise her young.

In this glut of springtime outdoor chores, this rush and return of summer wings, The Man realizes that everything seems so back-to-normal that he's almost forgotten his concern for Broken Wing. How long has it been since he last saw his rusty blackbird friend? Two weeks? More? Is he dead? Have other rusty blackbirds now returned? Has he rejoined the others of his kind, up in the bog above the house? Is he mating? Where is Broken Wing? What is happening?

Tree swallows fill the nesting boxes The Man has placed there for the bluebirds. The tree swallows love the bluebird boxes, and The Man loves the tree swallows. He loves to see the mother birds peeking their heads out of the round hole in the box, watching him move to and fro about this orchard and garden. Curious and wary, but not alarmed enough to leave the nest, the tree swallow mothers find this odd two-footed creature who can't fly an interesting diversion from the boredom of sitting on a clutch of eggs, or so The Man Who Lives Alone in the Mountains imagines.

And when the leaves on the apple trees are about the size of the end of his thumb, The

Man begins looking intently for the arrival of the summer warblers. Here they come, up from their wintering grounds in Mexico, Jamaica, Trinidad and Tobago!

Then, one early morning only a little after sunrise, as the man stands at the window looking out at the daily-more-burgeoning springtime, as he thinks about whatever it is he thinks about at times like these, he hears a little thud against a window at the other end of the house, and knows exactly what it means. Quickly, he goes outside, and there, beneath a window, is a beautiful myrtle warbler lying in the grass.

It saw the reflection of the trees beyond the house in the window, thought that was outdoors, too, and flew full-speed and headlong into the window. Luckily, this one is only stunned, and after the Man holds it in his hands for a while, he brings it inside to let it recover.

But now, while he has this tiny bird here in his hands, he looks at the bright yellow feathers on the back of its head and on its throat just under its chin; and on the sides of its breast, just in front of its folded wings; and on its rump, just where its tail feathers begin. And where these bright, intensely yellow places are not, the feathers are blue-gray—not gray, not blue, blue-gray—and a little black and white here and there in patches, too.

Oh, what a handsome and beautiful bird this myrtle warbler is!

He holds it in his hands until the little bird opens its black eyes and begins to blink—the first stage in its recovery. But The Man knows it is not ready yet to go back outside, so he waits until he feels its feet begin to paw and scratch at the palm of his hand where he has him cupped, loosely captured. As The Man opens his hands ever so slightly, the bird struggles more, and his eyes are blinking now more, too, as he begins to look around. Time to go back outside. The man places him carefully on an apple branch, where the bird clings tightly but still unsteadily. The Man stays with him for a little while, stroking his feathers back into place, unruffling them from his capture. Still, the bird does not fly; still, he is sick. Getting better, but still sick. The Man still stays with the little bird. Better not leave yet. Better not give a passing hawk or red squirrel a chance for an easy meal. Now the bird is perking up a little more, and now The Man is getting impatient, so he goes inside, but still keeps watch over his little friend. Then, suddenly—it is always suddenly—away the myrtle warbler flies, flies away into the spring day, into the rest of its life.

It's a busy day today, because not long after the myrtle warbler flies away, not long after the morning moves toward noon, at the kitchen window, suddenly—it is always suddenly—there is a buzzing, humming, squeaking sound.

Back again this year, and all the way from Mexico. Right there, just a windowpane away, this fiery little fellow rotating his wings so fast they are almost invisible, hovering there right in front of The Man's face, squeaking and honking that little beep. The tiny ruby-throated hummingbird, fearless, pugnacious and aggressive, announces his arrival here in this particular place again this year, demanding now that The Man get out his hummingbird feeders, make some nectar, and get ready for another summer. The Man obeys and hangs the little red, round feeders off the sides of the house and from the apple trees.

"That particular hummingbird who came just a little bit ago to the window," The Man thinks to himself, as he does every spring, "that particular bird *had* to have been here last year. He went to Mexico last fall, and has come back to this exact spot again this year. It has to be. If it were not so, how would he know to come to the window and announce his arrival?"

As The Man turns to go inside, he sees, swooping into an apple tree just to his left, a small flock of striking and beautiful rose-breasted grosbeaks. Now, added to the yellow, white and black evening grosbeaks who have been here all winter, here comes the rose-breasted grosbeak, shining with the throbbing colors of the mating season. The male struts his black back, white breast, and intense red bib-vest. He is a proud and beautiful addition to the dooryard.

In the evening now, and in the morning, The Man Who Lives Alone in the Mountains hears the loons fly over, calling their wailing, war-bling calls as they move back and forth from pond to pond.

It is a late May morning, and, although there is much to do outside, it is rainy and cold, so The Man sits down at his desk, takes pen and paper, and begins a letter to his friend.

Dear Howard,

Thank you for your last two letters. I haven't written in a while, so I thought I'd better get to it. More ornithology.

I saw a woodcock in the back yard about a week ago. I don't actually think I've ever seen a woodcock hunting for worms that close up or for such an extended period of time. I haven't been that close to one since maybe ten years ago, while I was mowing a roadside by hand with a gasoline-powered brush saw. I accidentally cut off the head of a female woodcock frozen on her nest. I was upset and saddened by what I'd done, but such things happen now and then. I didn't want to waste her, so I said a prayer for those four dark and light brown and gray speckled eggs that would never hatch, wrapped their mother's body up in some paper, put her in my lunch pail, and brought her home. I cooked her and ate her for supper that night. Woodcock eat mostly earthworms, and her flesh was very dark, moist, and tasted faintly like liver. She tasted good. And I was glad to have that beautiful, wild creature inside me.

As I was saying, I was inside the house about a week ago, looking out the window—I spend a lot of time looking out the window. She didn't know I was watching. That beak is long! And she jammed it into the ground again and again. I thought the ground was still more frozen than that, but apparently not. She was wonderful to watch, going about her business of getting something to eat. Trot, trot, trot—probe, probe. Trot, trot—probe, probe, probe. Trot, trot, trot, trot—probe. Trot—probe, probe. On she went along the side hill, doing her little wobble.

I knew I'd seen that behavior before somewhere. Then it dawned on me: sandpipers along the shoreline on the beach at the ocean. The identical, I mean identical, behavior. So I looked up the woodcock in my bird book. The same family: a sandpiper, grown much larger and moved inland to the swamps and marshes.

Howard, I think I could become a biologist or an ornithologist or an evolutionist if I were younger. I can see the headline: *Urban Jazz Musician Turns Orchardist then Ornithologist and Evolutionist*. How's that? Evolution is the miracle God sent to us. To see the connection between those little flocks of sandpipers scurrying along the beach at the ocean, hundreds of miles from here, and this solitary woodcock in my yard here in the mountains, miles from any real water, is a miracle. The killdeer is a shore bird, too, miles from any shore.

Just as we are connected, Howard, by our race—if there is such a thing as race—even though we live so far apart in such different places, you in the city, I in the mountains, we are yet and forever connected to each other, just as those sandpipers on the beach at the ocean are connected to the woodcock and the killdeer here in the mountains.

A few days later, I was out putting up some new birdhouses, and as I was coming up the slope above the lane, between the house and the road, where the side hill is steep and where the oldest apple trees are—the ones I still have to bring back to good health and productivity, up behind the old lilac bush—as I worked my way up through that ancient part of the orchard full of tumble-down apple trees, there, in a tangle of fallen apple trunks and branches, in the middle of a thicket of hard hack and red maple, as I weaved my way through this underbrush, as I put my left foot down on the sere, brown, springtime earth. There! Less than two inches from the outside of my left boot, a female woodcock rose up and flew away weakly a few yards up the hill, landed, and began running up the hill with her right wing outstretched, doing the old "broken wing trick" to lure me away.

I froze, hoping desperately that I had not actually stepped on her nest, but only near it. I looked down, and after searching for a long, long time, I saw, just a few inches from my left boot, four dark and light, brown and gray speckled eggs lying in a rude tangle of twigs and leaves. I moved carefully away from the nest, after noting equally carefully, or so I thought, its location.

The next day, I took a pair of binoculars to a place just up the hill from the nest. I knew—I mean, I thought I knew—exactly where the nest was, and in fact, I did know exactly; but nonetheless, even with binoculars, it took me forever to find her and the nest again, nestled as they all were in that flawless camouflage. Then—there she was.

Only her shiny, black eye gave her away. There she was, still as death, but for her gleaming black eye, alert and wide open and watching. Was she watching me?

Look at her, look at how beautiful she is. See the gray and many shades of brown patterned across her body. See those three or four dark brown lateral stripes on the top of her head. See her long bill. Four or five inches long! There, the shape of her round, compact body on the nest and her short, stubby tail sticking out the back.

And you must not, dare not, take your eyes off of her for even a moment, not a second, because, if you do, when you look back again to that exact spot, precisely where you looked before, she will have vanished, she'll be gone, melted into her surroundings without ever having moved a feather.

In that moment, it dawned on me that the mother woodcock was in a hurry here, for she is shades of brown and gray, and her eggs are brown and gray, also—meaning, I realized, that she must hatch and fledge her young *before* the world turns green and she and her eggs and their absolutely perfect camouflage aren't perfect anymore.

The next day, I went back again with my binoculars to that place up the hill from the nest, and again, with great difficulty, I found the nest in its brushy tangle, but no mother woodcock—only some shards of eggshell, and only two pieces of two eggs, the other eggs gone completely.

I've got a piece of one of those eggshells here on my desk.

I know the young can leave the nest just a few hours after hatching, but there was something about the way the eggs were broken, the way some of the eggs were missing entirely, that said to me things were not right.

A few nights earlier, in the middle of the night, I had switched on the porch light and seen, newly emerged from his winter's hibernation, a handsome skunk eating spilled sunflower seeds under the dooryard apple tree. Skunks like nothing better for dinner, I know, than a nest full of eggs.

Does this mother woodcock have the time to find a mate again, to get herself impregnated again? Does she have time to hatch and brood another clutch of eggs before the world turns green? Can she find a safe place for her eggs somewhere far from that skunk? Or must she wait until next spring to try again for babies?

This turn of events upset me more than it usually does. I know, as I said earlier, such things happen now and then; and besides, that skunk has more right to those eggs, I suppose, than I did to the body of the woodcock that I, albeit accidentally, beheaded all those years ago. But what at least seemed like the skunk's raid on the nest upset me greatly, nonetheless. I turned away from that place where there had been life in the making, where there had been the promise of new life, and where now, suddenly, just now suddenly, there was no life, and no promise of life, and came into the house.

Maybe it's the presence of my little friend here with me this winter, my pal Broken Wing, who I've been writing to you about. Maybe it's his struggle to hang on—he's doing quite well, by the way!—that has made me more aware than I usually am of how hard it is for some creatures to survive, especially creatures like Broken Wing who have so many strikes against them from the start: stranded in a strange and hostile season, put upon by predators, crippled almost to death. What more can happen to him while he still survives?

Some people are born with silver spoons in their mouths, and then have everything given to them, the way smoothed and paved for them before they even set out on their way; but there are a lot of the rest of us, most of us (almost all of us!) who don't. You and I both know plenty about this because of who we are, and what our place in this world has been and is. We both know more than we wish we knew about having strikes against us before we even begin. I see in Broken Wing my own struggle and my own life, our struggle and our lives.

Your friend,

Now, each morning, each warm morning before the sun, as The Man wanders between the rows of his newly-planted garden, two ravens, the sun's black acolytes, come croaking, crying: "Day!" Are they the same two who, last winter, hauled off all that bread?

Today, they saw him watching. They wheeled: the *hiss, hiss, hiss* of wings. Gone. They withered into the rising sun and left him standing, growing that day's dying shadow.

Emerging now in the garden, these strange potato plants, whose leaves emerge from underground already opened—as if they were some kind of deep-green aquatic plant that has lived at the bottom of this earthy sea, cut loose—rising now to the surface to float for a time in the air and sun.

And waiting for these new potato leaves to float to the top of this earthy sea, waiting and crawling about on the loose soil, the potato beetle waits for its life of devouring leaves.

Mid-June: almost the longest day of the year, and here in this northern place, in this short northern summer, where it is impossible to get too much warmth and light into one's body or one's life, The Man Who Lives Alone in the Mountains rises with the dawn on these delicate summer mornings. As he walks out across the dewy lawn with his cup of tea in his hand, heading toward the garden, he startles, stops, sees…what?

There, running up and down between the rows of potato plants just beginning to emerge…could it be? Yes…he sees…Broken Wing…and…another rusty blackbird the size of Broken Wing…and…and…two little rusty blackbirds. All of them scurrying intently, walking, running—as rusty blackbirds always prefer to do—up and down the rows of emerging potatoes, picking and eating potato bugs as earnestly and as quickly as they can.

Broken Wing is alive, and not only does he have a mate, the two of them have young. And here they are now, returning the kindness of The Man Who Lives Alone in the Mountains by picking his potato bugs for him!

The Man is so pleased to see them there, so grateful for their help and so touched by what he imagines to be their trust in him, that he, unthinking, advances on the little family as if to pick them up and say hello. Broken Wing and his family, of course, immediately scurry away, letting The Man know in no uncertain terms that this trust is at a distance, and is meant to stay that way.

The Man is touched and pleased and grateful for his friendship with Broken Wing and his

family, however distant it must be; yet The Man is also sad.

"What is wrong with me? We were meant to go two by two. All around me, now that it is spring, everyone comes in pairs; even Broken Wing has a partner. What is wrong with me? Why am I here in this place alone? Why have I exiled myself here, separated from my people, from my origin, from everyone? What's wrong with me?"

Now the tree swallow chicks fledge, and both the adults and the young swoop and twitter through the garden, eating insects caught on the wing in mid-air and on the ground. Oh, isn't The Man Who Lives Alone in the Mountains glad to have all these birds here helping him with his summer garden?

The hummingbirds and their young zoom and dart, loop and twirl through the apple trees, past The Man's head as he sits on his porch. They perform their acrobatic aerial displays all day long, drinking from the feeders, fighting and playing.

In the morning, when he steps outside with his cup of tea and walks across the dewy grass into the rows of his garden, as his vegetables awaken and yawn toward another summer day, and he sees Broken Wing and his family scurrying among the garden rows, eating insects, and the tree swallows twitter overhead, catching insects in the air, and the purple finches sing their intense and liquid songs, and robins cluck across the lawn, and mourning doves low, and chickadees scold; and above all, when the ravens have come from their lofty aeries to the east again this morning, to see what's changed since yesterday—and, oh, how they croak and chortle among themselves, editorializing on what The Man has done—and when, high above the ravens, the red-tailed hawk, who has left her nest to hunt—her nest, which is in the yellow birch, which hangs out over the waterfall just beyond the garden, where the deep woods begin—when the red-tailed hawk hunts and cries, and all those other birds sing, and The Man wanders among the rows of his various green friends stretching themselves into the summer, toward what they were meant to be, and the day dawns peaceful and calm and warm, then...The Man Who Lives Alone in the Mountains thinks about his life here in this place, thinks about his loneliness and how he moves through his days without another of his kind, and he smiles to himself, and says, "It's okay. Right now, at least, it's okay."

At times like these, The Man Who Lives Alone in the Mountains' whole self goes out of himself and into the birds, the trees, the sky, his vegetables, his apples, his grapes and blueberries, the chipmunks in the yard, the wild turkeys, the hawks, the deer and moose, the gravel in the driveway, even the red squirrels and woodchucks he has shot and killed; his self goes out of himself, and into all those things outside himself, and he loses himself. He disappears.

Broken Wing and his family are now almost a daily occurrence in the garden. Early each morning, they descend from the high, boreal bog above the house, and come into the garden and patrol up and down the rows, looking for bugs. Now that summer is wearing on and the cabbage worms have emerged on the broccoli, collard greens, and cabbages, Broken Wing and his family spend a little extra time each morning picking these very-nearly-invisible chartreuse parasites off the blue-green leaves so much the color of themselves that The Man marvels at how Broken Wing and his family can find the leaf-lopping interlopers.

Then, one late summer day in the middle of the afternoon, during a time when The Man Who Lives Alone in the Mountains is weeding and hoeing in his garden, at a moment when he has stopped to stretch his back and stand for a moment, resting on his hoe, The Man hears a faint rustling noise and feels the slightest breeze pass by his right ear. He turns his head ever so slowly and carefully to the right, toward where his right hand holds onto the hoe, and there, perching on top of the hoe handle, is Broken Wing! He is less than eighteen inches away, staring at The Man. The Man holds stock still. Only a smile moves across his face, broadening his mouth and narrowing his eyes. Then Broken Wing is into the air and away.

The Man thinks to himself that this little visit is a message—as if Broken Wing were saying, "You and I, my friend, can get a little closer than most birds and humans do, but when I am here with my family, no such thing can be."

The Man chuckles to himself as he wanders among his plants, inspecting their fruit and leaves, and sees the little dents Broken Wing and his family leave as they pick and peck the worms away. Make no mistake, The Man is not in any way complaining. He is grateful to his little rusty blackbird friend and his family for their help with his gardening, and he smiles to himself at this friendship he has with a bird.

Summer is waning now, and The Man Who Lives Alone in the Mountains sits on his porch in the dying afternoon, the angle of light grown more and more oblique as the afternoon turns toward evening. As he sits there, he looks out across this tiny place in the big world, and sees the tree swallows and barn swallows and their

litters of young, now grown almost to adulthood, swoop and twitter above and through the garden, catching a late-afternoon hatch of insects. And down the road, somewhere not too far away, a couple of the Bap Brothers' cows blat, and far off on the mountainside to the east, the faint sound of a chainsaw comes and goes as the afternoon's wind shifts direction.

All this music, all these songs. All these different kinds of songs. And there are other songs, as well.

The *kuk-kuk-kutuck* of a pileated woodpecker just beyond the pond, in his or her usual place, off into the woods, the same place year after year, the same place for a thousand years.

The guttural stammer of the ravens who live in the eastward mountains, and who daily come to see what The Man has done, how things have changed from the day before.

The shrill whistle of the red-tailed hawk, so high above the house she is invisible.

And there are the calls of the smaller, closer, more familiar summer birds. The white-throated sparrow's eleven-note song, saying: *old Sam Pea-bo-dy, Pea-bo-dy, Pea-bo-dy.* The similar three- and five-note songs of the chickadee, who sings: *dee-dee-dee, chick-a-dee-dee-dee; dee-dee-dee, chick-a-dee-dee.* The gurgle of the yellow throat down in the wet place below the garden. The cluck of a robin. The odd and beautiful, lowing squeak of the cedar waxwing. And down across the road in the pasture, the mellifluous and liquid warble of the bobo-link—this bird of the broadening fields who never comes near the house, since it is too close to the woods for this singer of open spaces.

And added to these songs, also, is the song The Man Who Lives Alone in the Mountains sings, his occasional little whistle in imitation of his airborne friends, his contribution to the ageless and eternal call and response, or some little bird cry or humming song of his own: far from the music he used to make with his friends in the city, but music nonetheless.

And beneath and among and above all this, always and constantly, that late-summer hum of insects, billions and billions of insects, all making their own individual species' sound, all crying, singing and crying their way toward their fall graves.

And thrown over this cornucopia of sound, as if it were a soft, translucent veil: the ever-present and delicate silence of the wilderness.

Then, abruptly fluttering down to land on the railing of the porch, here again is Broken Wing, come to stare at The Man Who Lives Alone in the Mountains as he sits alone on his porch. The Man says hello and asks the little bird how he is doing, how things are going up there in the bog above the house. He asks about his wife and children, and Broken Wing, as usual, doesn't answer, but simply looks at The Man with what seems to be a quizzical stare. Is it curiosity? Gratitude? Trust? The way Broken Wing cocks his head a little to the side. What?

The Man could see that the primary feathers on Broken Wing's right wing, which had jutted so sharply away from Broken Wing's body last fall, were disappearing now, and they were slowly being replaced by new feathers growing from his healing wing. Would Broken Wing be well enough, strong enough in another couple of months, to fly south with his family, with the rest of his kind? Or would he have to spend another winter in the north?

The air cools, and already, that autumnal cry of insects floats across the earth. These fleshy instants of a summer's day plant seeds during harvest time, trust their futures to the earth, and prepare to go away.

It is the end of summer, and the sun that stood high in the summer sky and baked The Man's head passes coolly now across his shoulders, as it slides down his back, as it slides down the sky, as it slides down the season, as it slides from north to the south, as it slides down the year toward winter.

Evening: when the day's birds are gone and the night's wanderers wait listening, when dark falls softly as a bird's wing; then, beyond the meadow in the bull spruce, a barred owl, this secretive bird of the deep woods, this bird The Man Who Lives Alone in the Mountains has listened to every summer for so long...the barred owl, another one alone, the barred owl, *alone, alone, alone,* begins his dark melody to the moon.

The year, this quick and momentary summer, this temporary interruption to the cold, tumbles down its long fall toward dark.

September. The dawn brings air thin and clear as cellophane. Under a cloudless sky, the frost passes through his garden that knew only sun and rain, a gentle people of leaves who ripened fruit all summer. All the life that was alive in leaves and stalks, fruit and flower: these plants wither now, droop, these glorious green plants that just yesterday were so full of juice and life are corpses now, their sudden and transitory lives gone. The garden is a grave.

Then rain. Red leaves turn white bellies to the wind. The year teeters perfectly on light's fulcrum: the equinox. Then it sinks. In a fog, it drowns as in a sea. The varying gray, the mist, shows each ridge, each spine of mountains as separate from the others, as if row upon row of granite breakers caught in a photograph, in perpetual stillness, might roll again, might make a primal, fog-bound ocean here—miles from any water.

Almost all the leaves are down. The popples turn yellow, and last the tamaracks, as well, in this northern place. Everything becomes gray—again. Again, the bare trees stretch their skinny fingers against the sky.

And the birds leave; his summer friends go away. Last night, the sky filled with geese, those voices high and strange and far away, who cry: *Good-bye! Good-bye!* The next day: forty degrees and rain. The earth shivers in its cloudy robe. Crows swarm and go.

Broken Wing, Broken Wing, where is Broken Wing? Alive or dead? Still here, or gone away? Broken Wing, Broken Wing, where is Broken Wing? Will I ever see you again? Broken Wing, Broken Wing, where are you, Broken Wing?

November again. Gray. Dark. Return. Chimney smoke lies down, crawls across the meadow like a slow, soft snake. The Man is done. His apples off to market, his woodshed full of wood, his little house banked tight against the cold, the cellar full of vegetables and apples, he comes inside and washes summer from beneath his fingernails.

Broken Wing, Broken Wing, where is Broken Wing? Alive or dead? Still here, or gone away?

In silence now, in the dying year, he darkens like the days. He sits and falls, as leaves fall, deeper into the coming dark, into that time to watch and wonder, into the time of dream. Quiet. Quiet. Still. In the darkening afternoon, he watches stove light flicker. The earth is empty again. The long night steps slowly over the mountains. The sky steals light from both ends of the day.

Broken Wing, Broken Wing, where is Broken Wing? Alive or dead? Still here, or gone away?

Another gray November passed into the snows and cold of another winter and winter merged into spring and spring into summer. The Man Who Lives Alone in the Mountains turned to his garden, planting peas and spinach, lettuce and the brassicas, and then potatoes. After about two weeks, the potato leaves emerged already unfurled from underground, as they always do, and there again this year were the potato bugs on the surface of the soil, just waiting for the leaves.

Early one late-June morning, as the night mists still hung in shreds like tatters of gossamer in the ravine below the garden, The Man walked to his garden to look around. There, to his surprise and delight, running up and down the rows of emerging potatoes, was a family of rusty blackbirds: a male, a female and three young. Both adults were indistinguishable from any other adult rusty blackbird. The Man looked hard at the right wing of the male bird, trying to see some sign of former injury. He could see none. As The Man approached the garden, the rusty blackbird family rose up and flew away.

Yet on many mornings the rest of that June and July, that family, or some family, visited the garden again and again to harvest insects.

Then, one mid-afternoon in early August as The Man sat on his porch taking a rest from his chores and finding relief from the midday sun, a rusty blackbird soared around the dooryard apple tree and landed on the porch railing. The Man froze, yet looked intently into the eyes of the rusty blackbird standing now on the porch railing. The rusty blackbird looked intently at The Man, also. Then, as suddenly as the rusty blackbird had arrived, he bounced up into the air and winged away beyond the trees.

9.
THE SPRING OF GRIEF

In the morning, The Man Who Lives Alone in the Mountains awoke slowly, and while he lay there with his eyes still closed, he began to plan his day, began to think about what more chores he had to do now that summer was on the wane and fall about to arrive.

He got out of bed, looked out the window and...what? He saw the world deep in snow. What? No. No. It can't be. It can't be!

Now, The Man Who Lives Alone in the Mountains realized that the time from when he had gone to bed last night, through the spring and summer—the summer life of Broken Wing and his family—through the following fall, through the next winter and spring, and into the next summer, to the moment when the rusty blackbird had landed on the porch railing that August afternoon eighteen months from the time he'd gone to sleep—all of it, all of it, all had been a dream.

How *could* it be a dream? How could he dream a year and a half of life in such detail? It seemed so real! Had he not seen Broken Wing and his family hunting insects in the garden? Had he not seen Broken Wing perched on the top of his hoe handle? Had he not seen spring, summer and fall all come and go? And winter and the next spring, also? Had he not seen the rusty blackbird, on that August afternoon, land on the porch railing and stare at him? Had that not been just yesterday? How could all that be only a dream?

Yet outside the window right now, it was not August. It was the morning after a late winter storm. Yes, that storm.

Yet, The Man wondered to himself, how could he know that this, too, this moment right now, wasn't also just a dream? When are we awake? When are we dreaming? How can we tell one from the other? His dream had seemed at least as real as his waking! How can we tell one from the other? Right now: am I awake or am I dreaming?

He moved into his living room and to the wood stove, where he started the morning fire.

The storm of the day and the night before had passed. The barometer was high again. The new day dawned clear and bright and calm, as if yesterday and last night had never visited this place. Yet one look out the window gave evidence of the storm's passing and effect. A new landscape shone bright under the morning sun.

The Man got dressed for the out-of-doors. He had to lean hard against the storm door to move it even a little against the two feet of snow piled against it. When he had opened it enough to squeeze out, he worked his way to the woodshed door, opened it, and stepped into the snowless woodshed, where he found his shovel. And as he did these things, he had a feeling he'd just done these things. He knew he'd just done these things. He felt confused, disturbed.

As he went about digging out from the storm—there must have been somewhere between two and three feet of new snow—his attention and worry turned to Broken Wing.

He dug new paths to the dooryard feeders, cleaned them off, and filled them up with seeds. With his tractor, he plowed the lane—filled in during the night from bank to bank with snowdrifts—down to the road.

Then The Man came inside and made a cup of tea and ate his breakfast. And all the time, all he could think about was Broken Wing. Was he still alive? And if he was, where was he?

Slowly, the birds descended from the softwood thickets above the house and returned to the feeders. First the chickadees, then the nuthatches, then the downy and hairy woodpeckers; then a flock of evening grosbeaks swooped in, announcing with showy aplomb that they, too, had made it through the night. All morning, The Man watched for a medium-sized rusty blackbird. He watched and worried.

Morning passed into afternoon, afternoon into evening. The Man kept going to the window to look out at the feeders, hoping to see his little rusty blackbird friend, but Broken Wing did not appear.

He cooked and ate his dinner listlessly. That evening, he tried to distract himself with reading. Nothing would do. Where was Broken Wing? Surely, if he had survived last night, he would have appeared somewhere, sometime, today.

Evening and night and the next morning, and still no Broken Wing. All that day passed, and The Man Who Lives Alone in the Mountains did little else but watch out the window.

"If only I'd captured him the day of the storm, down there under the white spruce tree! He was within arm's reach! I could have grabbed him. I know he would have let me. Why didn't I save him from his own wildness? I could have put him in my pocket, or carried him in my hands, up out of that storm. I could have brought him inside, put him in the cage. Just for one night. If I had done that, he would be alive today! This is all my fault. I am to blame. I should have saved him. Why didn't I help him? Where was I when he really needed me? Why didn't I help him?

"Or what if I had captured him, and had him cupped in my hands, and was struggling through the blizzard back toward the house when he began to squirm, trying to get free of my clutches—what if he'd done that, and had gotten away, and then was out there stranded in the storm, with no protection at all? If that had happened, I most certainly would be to blame for his death. What if that had happened?"

The days passed into weeks, and still no sign of Broken Wing.

The Man gave up hope. His dream of Broken Wing's survival and prosperity had been a false prophecy, to be sure. "My dream deceived me. Wishful thinking and true prophesy are not the same thing," he said to himself.

The Man Who Lives Alone in the Mountains knew that Broken Wing was dead.

Yet every morning, when The Man woke up, after the birds got up and began to move about in the dooryard, he still watched out the window, waiting and hoping that by some miracle, Broken Wing might appear. But Broken Wing never did appear.

The deep snows of winter were shrinking fast now, and The Man had begun going every day down to where the white spruce tree stood alone in the little meadow below the house, to look for the body of Broken Wing. Every day, sometime during the day, he made his way down there to look around. He wanted desperately to find the body of his little friend before someone else, some scavenger, did.

Then, one day, as the snows of winter shrunk under a warm rain, there he was, revealed by the melting snow: the frozen body of Broken Wing preserved perfectly, not far from where The Man had left him the evening of the storm.

The Man picked him up and carried him into the house and laid him down carefully on the mudroom floor. He got a large, airtight plastic bag from the kitchen, came back to the mudroom, put Broken Wing in the plastic bag, sealed it, and put the bag with the dead bird in it in the freezer. When spring was fully here, when the ground had thawed, when summer was on the verge, he would bury his little friend.

Now all but the last patches of the winter snow were gone. Now only here and there, hiding in those shaded and dark north-sloping dingles, did there remain a little declivity of dirty snow littered with twigs, bark, hemlock needles and cones, and the other detritus of winter. Yet, even now, two months since The Man had found the body of Broken Wing, even now, sometimes the burgeoning spring sunlight would fall at a certain angle on a blue jay at the feeder, so that the blue jay looked black. Then The Man's breath caught in his throat as he stared out the kitchen window in the morning, waiting for the water for his tea to boil, and he would think he saw Broken Wing. But Broken Wing was never there. All spring, again and again as he moved through his springtime chores in his apple orchard, there would come a moment when The Man's heart stopped as he thought he saw Broken Wing out of the corner of his eye, flitting into a tree.

That was a sad spring for The Man Who Lives Alone in the Mountains. Everywhere he went, he expected to see, wanted to see, Broken Wing, even though he knew the body of the bird lay in his freezer.

Dear Howard,

Gray and rain and chill here today. Oh, how I love this cold rain, this gray spring. I love the chill that keeps me indoors and the fire going in the stove all day. I love this last nod toward the passing cold and dark. I love all that is depressed and sad and sullen. I love all that is empty, slothful and withdrawn. Summer yesterday, the end of winter today, just right for the way I feel, just right for a letter to you.

I buried Broken Wing yesterday.

Spring is here, at least it was yesterday. It was a beautiful, a perfect, spring day. The sun was high and warm, the birds, just returned from their wintering grounds, were alive with song, everything was swollen with the juice and hum and song of new life. What better day than one like that for a funeral?

And the ground is finally thawed. So I went out to my workshop in the woodshed and built a little box just big enough for him out of some half-inch stock of white pine I had up in the rafters. I even hinged the lid. A little coffin for my little friend. I made a little sign out of the same half-inch stock of white pine, and nailed it to a stick. Then I went around the place, over the side hill, and gathered up some stones. I dug a little grave out at a far corner of the garden, so he could be close to all those garden insects he went after so diligently in my dream.

I came inside and got Broken Wing out of the freezer and put him in the little coffin, took the coffin out to the grave, and put it in. I covered him over and filled in the grave; then I used the stones to make a little stone cairn to cover over the earth-scar, and also to keep off the grave robbers like the skunks. I drove the little sign on its stick into the ground just behind the stone cairn. The sign said:

Here Lies

BROKEN WING
† † † † † † †

A
Small and Brave
Life

Then I read a little poem over the grave. A little coffin, a little grave, a little cairn, a little sign, a little poem... for my friend.

I read D. H. Lawrence's:

SELF PITY

I never saw a wild thing
sorry for itself.
A small bird will drop
frozen dead from a bough
without ever having felt
sorry for itself.

That's out of *The Complete Poems of D. H. Lawrence* that you gave me all those years ago; do you remember? That huge book of his poems, 965 pages of poems, and from a novelist. I don't think there could be a more appropriate poem for Broken Wing.

Then I sang a song, a little ditty, I made up:

Broken Wing, Broken Wing, where is
* Broken Wing?*
Alive or dead? Still here or gone away?

Broken Wing, Broken Wing, where is
* Broken Wing?*
Alive or dead? Still here or gone away?

Broken Wing, Broken Wing, where is
* Broken Wing?*
Broken Wing, Broken Wing, will I ever
* see you again?*

Broken Wing, Broken Wing, where are
* you Broken Wing?*
Broken Wing, Broken Wing, here you
* are my friend,*

Buried in this ground. Alive or dead?
* Dead, oh, dead.*
And never will I see you again, Broken
* Wing.*

And never will I see you again, Broken
  Wing.
Broken Wing, Broken Wing, where are
  you Broken Wing?

The ceremony was short, and I was the only one there. I'm glad I did it. Maybe I've been up here in this mountain wilderness living alone too long. Do you think I'm crazy for having a funeral for a bird?

On my way back to the house after the burial, I remembered a poem by Ikkyu, that 15th-century Japanese poet, which goes:

I found my sparrow Sonrin
Dead one morning
And dug his grave as gently
As I would my own daughter's.

Maybe if I hadn't spent my life alone in this lonely place, maybe if I had married and had had a daughter, I might not be so obsessed with a bird, or feeling so sorry for myself, either. But I didn't, and I am.

Maybe D. H. Lawrence is right. Maybe birds never do feel sorry for themselves, but men do, especially this man right now. I'm having a hard time this spring. I can't seem to get that little bird out of my mind. Not that I'm trying all that hard. Actually, I think I'm not trying at all to forget; rather, I'm trying to remember, to cling to the memory of that small life.

There is something about Broken Wing's life and his death, and our time together before his death, that's become some kind of symbol, a sign or something, for me. There is something in his life and death that draws me to him.

And it's not pity, either. I learned a lot about the uselessness of pity this past fall and winter. It's something else, something about how well he struggled, how strongly he resisted, how courageously he fought. Maybe it's courage I'm talking about. I don't know. There is something in Broken Wing's life and death that is important to me.

And it's not just courage. It's resistance, too. A will to fight, fight back; struggle and not give up, survive. Maybe that's it.

Oh, I know, people will say there is no will here, no fight or resistance, or anything conscious at all. They will say there is only instinct. They will say that Broken Wing was just unconsciously following his instincts; that he didn't actually know or decide to struggle, fight, resist. So what? Call it what you will! He still did what he did for whatever reason or instinct that drove him on. I know I can't read a bird's mind, and I know everyone thinks these so-called lower creatures are unconscious, but I'm not so sure. I lived with that bird day in and day out, lived with his struggle to live, for all those months, every day, and all

I can tell you is: I could swear I could see in his eyes, in his body and his life, a conscious—I mean conscious in the way you or I would be conscious—a conscious struggle to stay alive, to survive, to stay here and live.

His life and death haunt me, Howard. They are with me constantly. I need to find some way to do something about all this, with all this, but I don't know what that something is.

Maybe it's the weather today, or burying Broken Wing yesterday; I don't know what it is, but something has gotten me thinking about the deaths of other birds I've known. It's like all these other bird deaths are marching through my mind today, a parade of deaths.

I spent a long time earlier today remembering a scene I'd witnessed years ago up in northern Canada: on a lake, a big lake, a lake with hundreds of miles of shoreline and thousands of islands in it. I was up there fishing, camped out on one of the islands. Early one morning, very early, just after sunrise—which, at that latitude, was about 4:30 at that time of the summer—I climbed out of the tent, built a fire, boiled some water for tea, made my tea, and went out onto a little jut of rock that stuck out into the bay on the island where I was camped. I remember I was all bundled up. It was summer, but it was cold; it might have been in the forties. I was sitting on this jut of rock, just watching dawn break. There were some herring gulls in the air and on the water, a few loons calling in the distance somewhere, and maybe a great blue heron behind me in the back of the bay.

Suddenly, a bald eagle came barreling into view from out of nowhere, and hit one of those herring gulls that was on the wing square on the back so hard, it knocked the gull out of the sky and into the water. Before the eagle had time to dive down and hit the gull again, all the other gulls began crying and harassing the eagle, the way little nesting birds do crows, and crows do owls. Within seconds, there were, there must have been, a hundred gulls, maybe more, in the air over that bay, crying and screaming and attacking the eagle.

But it was as if the eagle didn't even see all those gulls. The eagle dove down again and hit the wounded gull, who was now floundering on the water. Then the eagle rose up and dove, again and again and again, each time hitting the now-helpless gull with his talons as hard as he could. By now, one of the gull's wings was splayed out across the water, and with the other wing and his feet, the gull was trying desperately to paddle away from the attacking eagle; but he could get nowhere.

Again and again, the eagle dove and hit the gull. Over and over, he pummeled the gull. It was a messy scene. More and more, now, there were blood and feathers all around the gull. People think large predatory birds like hawks and eagles swoop in, grab their prey, kill it—and that is that. Wishful thinking is what that is. This whole attack and killing took the better part of twenty minutes to complete.

At some point, the hundreds of gulls who had been circling and diving and crying in the air could see that the wounded gull was beyond hope, and as suddenly as the gulls had arrived, they all disappeared. I wonder if they had been there to save the gull, or just to be with the gull as it died. Maybe they knew full well it was hopeless from the start. Maybe they knew the eagle would have his way. Maybe they stayed there, circling and crying, just to keep the wounded gull company as it died. Which makes me think of Broken Wing, and how he had to die alone. Well, in the end, the hundreds of gulls left, and the wounded gull died alone, just as Broken Wing died alone; just as you and I will die alone, also. That last job we do is a lonely one any way you slice it, no matter how many people or birds are around.

After the gulls left, the cacophony of their cries left, also; and the silence they left behind was frightening, because now I could hear the eagle plummet to the water, hear the impact of the eagle on the now hopelessly wounded gull, splayed out and bleeding on the water. Again and again, the eagle pummeled the gull, and each time he hit the gull, I could hear the thud of the impact. He'd hit the gull so hard the gull would go under water from the force of the blow, then bob back to the surface. By now, the gull couldn't even make a pretense at trying to paddle away somewhere. It just twitched and shivered there on top of the water.

Finally, when the eagle had decided that the gull was near enough to dead and beyond any ability to resist, the eagle came down much more slowly than he'd ever done before, grasped the gull in his talons, and laboriously rose up into the air. He got about twenty feet into the air and lost hold of the gull, which fell limply back onto the water. Again, the eagle came down, took hold, and took off, and again lost his grip, and again the gull fell to the water, and again the eagle came down, took hold and took off; and this time, winged off across the bay to an island on the far side with his breakfast.

I watched where the eagle headed, and later that morning, I took the boat and outboard, and went over to the bay into which I thought I'd seen the eagle glide. After a lot of looking around, I found a rock at the water's edge, some feathers, a few bloody bones, and two gull feet—nothing else.

As bloody and difficult as the slaughter of that herring gull that day had been, there was something inevitable about it. As upsetting as such a thing is to watch, it is not wanton, meaningless, or cruel. In the end, it was the preparation and consumption of a meal, and little more.

The way that bald eagle killed the herring gull that morning made me think, for some reason, of all the pheasants and quail I killed when I was a boy and lived on the farm and went hunting in the fall. The deaths of those pheasants and quail were somehow linked in my mind to the death of that gull. I, like the eagle, intended to kill them—for sport, yes, of course, but for food, also. I wonder if the eagle knows a sense of sport as well as food when he kills a gull or catches a fish. In any case, for both the eagle and for me, there was some kind of usefulness in those deaths. We got to eat them because we killed them.

Before I was old enough to use a shotgun and go after game birds, I had a BB gun, and I, like all the other boys around there, learned to hunt by hunting and killing songbirds, which has got to be different from the eagle killing that gull or my older self, killing pheasants and quail. I know Indian kids learned to use their bows and arrows by killing songbirds, also, but still, thinking back on all of that, it doesn't seem right. Yet killing all those songbirds with a BB gun

or bow and arrow doesn't bother me all that much. We were all learning to hunt. It bothers me, but not that much—not as much as the time I killed a great horned owl. I've never told anyone this story before. Never.

I was hunting squirrels down on the farm in the fall, down along the river that ran through our place. I was maybe sixteen. It was a warm, sunny autumn afternoon. I was working my way slowly up the river, sycamore trees on my left hanging out over the river and a mixed stand of oak and beech trees on my right. Some of my parents' corn and soybean fields were less than a hundred yards away, beyond the oaks and beeches. It was a kind of paradise for squirrels: plenty of water in the river, nuts in the beeches and oaks, and corn and soybeans nearby, as well. For some reason, I wasn't seeing any squirrels that day. Probably it was because it was the middle of the afternoon, and all the squirrels were asleep in their leaf nests, high up in those oak and beech trees.

I'd been hunting up the river for some time when I looked up through a kind of tunnel of trees, and there, about twenty yards ahead of me, on a low branch of a sycamore tree, sat a great horned owl looking right at me, right there in the middle of the day. Why he was out in the middle of the day, this night wanderer, I'll never know; but there he was, just

sitting there on that branch. He just sat there and looked at me.

I put my shotgun to my shoulder, aimed, and fired. He fell backward off the branch like a wad of dough falling from the kitchen counter to the floor. He didn't flutter or squirm. He just fell over and hit the ground and lay there.

I came up to him, and he was dead, completely dead. He wasn't twitching at all. He was big, much bigger than I imagined he would be, but when I picked him up to look at him, he was also much lighter than I imagined he would be. Birds are always lighter than they seem. I picked him up, and when I did, his head fell backward, totally limp, as if his neck were broken. All of him was limp, dead.

One shot had killed him. One wanton, meaningless shot had killed him. What was it in me that had made me do that? What purposeless, random, destructive part of me had killed that bird? Did I kill him just so I could look at him, touch him, pick him up?

The little boy in me who'd killed all those songbirds could almost be excused from his actions, even though he knew what he was doing was wrong. For him, it was the adventure of the hunt, those old, those ancient urges rising up in that little boy. And he was young; maybe he didn't completely know, quite yet, that what he was doing was wrong. But the murder of that owl was another matter.

There was no hunt involved. The boy wasn't little anymore, and he knew better; he knew clearly that what he was doing was wrong. Yet he did it anyway. That dark urge, that urge to kill just for the sake of killing, for the fun of killing—I carry that around inside of me all the time. I still do.

That moment was more than forty years ago, and I can still see it, to this day, as clearly as if I were there, at this moment. I can feel what kind of day it was, what the sky was like, how the sky looked up through and above the branches and leaves of those huge, old sycamore trees. I can smell the day. I can hear the river, and I can see that great horned owl sitting on that branch. I can see myself putting the gun to my shoulder, aiming, firing. I can see the owl falling to the ground. I can see myself standing over the owl, bending over, picking up the bird. I can see myself standing there, holding that big, dead bird, its head dangling limply off its shoulders.

I've also been thinking of other wanton deaths, not as deliberate as the death of the great horned owl, but no less useless and stupid.

Last summer, I came around the back corner of the house, and there, lying on the ground, was a black-billed cuckoo. It had been dead for days. Another meaningless accident. Another death caused by my desire to look out a window. I've been listening to black-billed cuckoos for thirty years in this place, and I'd never seen one until that day. You know, they are so secretive. I used to try to sneak up on them and get a look at them. I'd follow the call to where it was, being as stealthy as I could be, and when I got to where I heard it, it would be just ahead of me on the right. Then I'd sneak up there, and it would be just ahead of me on the left. Clearly, the cuckoo knew I was stalking it, and it was playing with me. It would move off just far enough so I couldn't get a look at it, but then it would stop and call to me to tease me. After many futile attempts to glimpse a cuckoo, I gave up. Now, I just listen to them, and I'm grateful.

I'm grateful especially to the few cuckoos who nest and breed around here, because cuckoos eat enormous amounts of insects. They especially like caterpillars of any kind, so in the years when a tent caterpillar infestation threatens my orchard, the cuckoos are especially welcome and useful. Often, in those years, I've thought, surely, this summer, I'll get a look at one, since they spend so much time in the apple trees foraging for caterpillars; but I've never seen one, never in all these years—never, that is, until last summer.

The constant, unseen presence of the black-billed cuckoo makes me think of all the other things that are all around us all the time that we never see. And of course, I admire the secretive, reclusive, retiring and shy manner with which the cuckoo goes about her life. Actually, when you think about it, the cuckoo is shy and retiring the way a rusty blackbird is. And somebody else I know, too.

She was such a beautiful bird, and much bigger than I thought she'd be. I think it was a female. I knew it was an adult, because the eye ring was quite red. Their tails are long and wonderfully constructed. Their tails are made of a series of pairs of feathers, each pair a little longer than the previous pair, and laid on top of the previous pair. Five or six pairs—each gradually longer than the pair beneath.

I picked up the dead cuckoo and put her on the compost heap out by the garden. Might as well get some good out of her.

While I'm burdening you with stories of useless and stupid bird deaths, I want to tell you about the influx of white-winged crossbills we had this winter. There's an allegory in this story, too.

The last couple of winters here, we've had high numbers of white-winged crossbills. This is a boreal bird if there ever was one. It lives almost exclusively on spruce cone seeds, and thus must go wherever they are in abundance. They'll eat tamarack and hemlock seeds, too—those being boreal trees, also. And, get this: if the spruce cone crop is especially large, they will even nest, lay eggs, hatch and raise young right in the middle of the winter. Food supply, my man—food supply is *everything*! Those of us who know about what people call the "inner city" know about that. Well, not *everything*. If food supply were everything, I wouldn't be so lonely.

This winter, even more than last, we've had large crops of spruce cones on both the red and white spruce trees around here. From a distance, the tops of the spruce trees look like they are dying; but it's just the red-brown of huge cone clusters covering the branches, and because of that bumper crop of spruce cones and the seeds inside them, crossbills seem to be everywhere, which becomes a serious problem when you're in a car going down the road.

Crossbills are birds of the far north, of wilderness places, and because they are such wild birds, they are tame, unused to people and cars; and therefore, they don't know to get out of the way when they are in the road looking for gravel and salt. For some reason, crossbills love salt.

This winter, one day I was coming back up the road from the valley and the village, and I saw what seemed like two little knots of dirty ice, or maybe small rocks in the road. Then, as I was upon those dark spots, I realized they were white-winged crossbills foraging in the gravel for what little bits of salty ice might have fallen off of cars. It wasn't until I was practically on top of them that they began to rise up and try to fly away. One of them made it; the other hit the grill of the car and came up over the hood, a disheveled ball of feathers, floating up over the windshield and the roof of the car. I pulled to the side of the road and stopped, got out, and went back to where the mortally wounded cross-bill was now lying in the road. I picked him up. His heart was beating fast, his chest heaving up and down just as fast. It seemed to me as if he were actually panting. His eyes were open. I thought about wringing his neck to put him out of his misery. It would have been the kind thing to do, and I've done it many times to mortally wounded pheasants and quail, but I couldn't bring myself to do it—even though I knew, or thought I knew, that I should. I smoothed off a little place for him on top of the snowbank along the side of the road, and laid him down. His eyes were still open, and he was still breathing, panting, very fast. I stayed with him. After a while, the breathing and panting slowed down a little, and then stopped.

What is death, Howard? There he was one moment, a white-winged cross-bill in the middle of the road picking up some salt, and all of a sudden, he's flying through the air, not with his wings, but as a wrecked ball of feathers floating up and over a car, then landing with a little soft thud on the snowy road. A creature comes along, picks him up, and places him on a snowbank, which is where his life ends.

What is death? How can he be that gorgeous little collection of feathers and flesh one moment, and an inert bit of matter the next? How can that be? What is it that made him alive? Surely, it is more than blood, a beating heart, muscle and instinct.

It's not the body. That body, inert now on the grimy snowbank, will sink into the earth there beside the road and rot, go back into and to earth, go back to where it came from. The body never dies, it just changes its form, from a beautiful collection of feathers and flesh to soil. That's not death; that's just transformation.

So, then, what is it that dies? His spirit, that one particular white-winged crossbill's spirit? Is that what dies? Or does it just leave that body there on the grimy snowbank, and fly away somewhere and enter some other white-winged crossbill's body, one in an egg about to be born? Or does it fly away and enter me, become part of me?

When death is, what dies? What is life? What is death that in a moment, there is no life where life was?

All this brooding on the death of birds didn't begin with today's gloomy weather. It began yesterday, in all that beautiful weather, and because of what happened to me out in the woods.

After I buried Broken Wing and had the ceremony, I went for a walk in the woods. This is an especially good time of the year to walk in the woods around here. The first few rounds of wildflowers are in bloom, but none of the understory has sprung up yet to crowd the forest floor, so the shape of the land is clearly visible, the way the ledge rock rises and falls and contours the earth; it's all there to see. And the trees are only just beginning to leaf out, so the sky is still there in abundance above the still, almost naked branches. Only the slightest hint of delicate green, that first and pale green of the leaves as they begin to unfurl, makes the beginning of a smoky-green haze in the branches of the hardwood trees.

And also, and especially, it is a good time to walk in the woods because the bugs aren't out yet. No no-seeums, no blackflies, no mosquitoes, no deerflies. It's bugless and wonderful out there for those few scant weeks, when the snow is mostly gone and the bugs haven't hatched yet.

Well, such a day it was yesterday, which is why I decided to take a walk in the woods after I buried Broken Wing. I thought it would be good for me, a balm for my soul, something, perhaps, to make the wounded whole.

I worked my way through the ravine out behind the garden, past the waterfall, past the big yellow birch where the red-tailed hawk nests most years. I was a few hundred yards out beyond that when I came to an old, hollow-cored beech tree I know well, a den tree for many over the years.

And there, at the base of that tree, in a hollow place in the trunk, the entrance to the inner empty core, where the roots go in, there—a raccoon, her chin resting softly on her crossed paws, her eyes wide open, looking straight ahead. Dead.

And somewhere else, unseen to me but not far from there, last year's fawn, having endured this whole and harsh winter, that last and final storm, having endured all that—she, just a couple of weeks ago, sought out a southern slope and lay her starved body down and died in the warming sun.

In spring, the earth is pimpled with the dead: dead raccoon, dead yearling deer, ruined woodcock eggs, Broken Wing's body rotting back into earth, another black-billed cuckoo somewhere beneath a window, the white-winged crossbill and all those other car-killed birds, rotting now beside the grimy, gravel-strewn road. All fertilizer now. Done. Gone.

In spring, when the earth is soft again and new;
in spring, when Earth says to Sun: *Come, seed*. In spring, those corpses are her seething body's rotting, phosphorescent jewels.

All gone. All done. No matter. Make more now,
make more of everything, with earth and rain and sun.

No stopping spring. No matter how much death there is—no stopping spring. Not now. Not ever.

What is death, Howard? What is life?

How can the one rise so joyfully and new out of the decaying body of the other?

Your friend,

10.
THE SUMMER
OF MOURNING

No matter how glum and brooding The Man Who Lives Alone in the Mountains was that spring, spring did what it always does: it burst in upon the stiff, winter world of ice and death, and turned everything flexible and green, and did it with an extravagance and burgeoning excess only spring knows how to muster.

The The Man tried to join this springtime parade of life, but it was difficult. Everywhere he went, he thought he saw Broken Wing flitting into the dark trees. Every thought he had seemed always to be interrupted by a thought of Broken Wing.

His vegetable garden, to which he devoted more love and attention than he had his apple trees, and almost as much love and attention as he lavished on the birds, seemed this summer to offer little help or distraction from his grief. In the past, his summer garden had always been such a pleasure for him. All those summertime vegetables, and the process of raising them: The Man had hoped the garden would be not only a pleasure, but a solace; but this year, it had turned out to be neither.

Rather, this summer, every time he saw a bug on a stalk of broccoli or a tomato plant or on his fence of peas, he saw Broken Wing chasing after it. And then he didn't see him.

Every morning, with his cup of tea in hand, when the Man went to the garden to look around, Broken Wing wasn't there; nor did he land on the hoe handle as The Man rested from his weeding and cultivating; nor on the railing of the porch as The Man ate his lunch. And when The Man walked up the hill above the house and along the logging road that runs beside the bog, Broken Wing wasn't there, either.

That June, in the garden, as he thought about Broken Wing and his midwinter night's dream, as time passed, his grief for the bird did not lessen, but instead grew stronger.

The more The Man actually lived through the events that had also been a part of his midwinter night's dream, the harder it became to endure them without the presence of Broken Wing. It was as if Broken Wing were a ghost at all the events he should have been present for in his living self. It was as if Broken Wing were a ghost in this entire summer of no Broken Wing; as if he should be living out the life he had had in the dream.

Then, late in June, two gifts of a sort—visitations, you might call them, from the avian world—began to help The Man adjust to the absence of his dead friend. And these gifts, these visitations, helped The Man feel encouraged, alive, even if only slightly, for the first time in a long time. He sat down one afternoon in his rocker on the porch, put his writing board across the arms of the rocking chair, and began a letter.

Dear Howard,

I've been meaning to write to you, but as you know, I've been in a funk since spring. But a couple of things have happened lately that have helped me rise up, even if just a little, out of my indigo mood.

I've been meaning to write to you for weeks to tell you about my white-throated sparrow friend with whom I've been playing duets every morning.

It all started early in June. There's a large balsam fir about halfway down the lane to the road. A few weeks ago, early one morning as I was headed to the road, I heard that distinctive call of the male white-throated sparrow. So I called back—I mean, I whistled back. I mean, I tried to. His call is so clear and pure and high that I had great trouble getting into his range and key. But I'm getting ahead of myself.

Let me get behind myself.

Before I go on, I want to tell you about a little poem I read not long ago, a haiku by Richard Wright. Yes, that's right, Richard Wright; the author of *Native Son, Black Boy, The Outsider, Black Power* and a collection of speeches almost no one's heard of called *White Man, Listen!* Here it is:

Leaving its nest
The sparrow sinks a second,
Then opens its wings.

That's *exactly* right! That's what happens. Details. Details are so important!

Back to where I was.

That first day, the first day when I heard him calling his call from high up in that balsam fir and I called back to him, much to my surprise and delight, he came barreling out of the branches of the tree and across the lane and into the old lilac bush on the other side, where he landed and called again. I called again, too, and he flew back to the balsam and called again. So I called again, also, and he again, as well. This time, he headed for the lilac again but stopped short of it, wheeled around, and came straight at me. I was standing in the middle of the lane. He flew around me several times, trying to figure out what kind of odd-looking and monstrous white-throated sparrow I was, and then back he went to his singing perch in the balsam fir.

Clearly, he was plenty irritated with me for my intrusion into what he considered *his* territory, and he'd come out to challenge me. Understanding this, I hollered, "Hey! I've been here 30 years! You just moved in last week!" Such logic meant little to him, and he came at me again, going back and forth from tree to lilac to tree as I began again walking down the lane to the road. I think he took my movement away from him as a sign of my retreat and his victory in this territorial battle, and I was not about to disabuse him of that notion. That was the extent of our encounter on that first day.

The next day and the next, and any day it wasn't raining, I'd go down on the lane and call to him—and he'd not only answer, but come out to challenge me. Slowly, I do believe, he got used to me, and I to him, and he quit acting so territorial. He grew tolerant and patient with me, and with my inability to pitch my song into his range. Sometimes, I could almost get into his octave, but never quite. The best I think I ever did was almost getting there, perhaps a third, sometimes a fifth, below him; yet even though I was singing harmony, he'd respond, and on those days, when I had to call in unison but a whole octave below, he'd still sing with me. I was grateful for what I saw as his graciousness and magnanimity, his patience, with my inabilities. Therefore, I was always careful, or as careful as I could be, to whistle his song with the proper intervals, even if I wasn't in the proper key. It seemed to me he didn't mind so much if I sang in F# while he sang in B, just so long as I got the intervals right. After all, change the intervals of a white-throat's song just slightly, and suddenly, you're a chickadee!

We came, I believe, to enjoy our morning duets. And I noticed, over the days we played together, that he often changed pitch and key. He had more than one way to sing his song. I wouldn't say we were exactly improvising together, but we also didn't do the same tune every time, either. It was music, Howard, that the two of us made there each morning together, and it pleased me. And, as I said, my guess is he didn't mind it too much, either.

And also this. The two of us there together every morning were the absolute-and-original-never-more-basic call and response. You know, it's odd. People think our music is urban, something generated in big cities; but everything about it began in the country, whether it was in Africa or here in our own South.

Call and response is probably the most obvious example of it all, and obviously our musical ancestors learned this way of playing from listening to the birds.

In a way, Howard, even though it seems I am about as far away from our music and our people as I could possibly get, what I've really done, I believe, is go back to the source, to the beginning of our music. Maybe that's another thing that keeps me here.

White Throat is gone now, and I wonder why. I wonder—no doubt because of the gloomy pallor hanging over me this spring—if he died, or was killed by the damn red squirrels that attack everything around here. Or maybe it was just that he and his mate, as soon as the chicks fledged, got out of here to be away from that lousy amateur musician in the neighborhood who was always trying to sit in, and then when he did get a chance to blow, played clams all the time. I'll never know why he left. All I know is he's not there anymore, and the silence isn't as pleasing as his song.

I miss him. Every morning as we sang, he'd display himself to me. His clear, brilliant white throat, and the bright yellow spot beside his eye, shown in the morning sunlight. He was a handsome little fellow. His kind has always meant spring to me. Winter is interminably long here. Yet when spring does come, and the robins and crows, the great migration of warblers, and all manner of other birds return, it doesn't really seem like spring until I hear the white-throated sparrows sing. When I hear that little song, then I know for sure spring has really come. I always think what they are saying with their song is

The sun! The sun! I bring the sun
In the bright spot beside my eye.
Come out! Come out of your house!
The sun has come!

Well, what that little white-throated sparrow didn't know was that his willingness to sing duets with me was the beginning of my return to the land of the living.

Howard, truly:

There is a balm in Gilead
    To heal the wounded soul.
There is a balm in Gilead
    To make the wounded whole.

And that balm—need I tell you?—is music.

I hope White Throat will return next year, and if not him, then perhaps his son or daughter, so that next June, I will have someone with whom to sing.

That's the first thing.

The second thing is: for the past ten days or so, there has been a crow hanging around here in the dooryard, actually in the yard, and out around the garden, too. He's got a club foot. His left foot is deformed. The claws, toes, and talons turn in, curl under, just as you'd expect, as you'd imagine. And he limps, as you'd also imagine he would. He has to walk on those knuckles. He seems to be able to fly alright, up to a tree, and perch okay; though he seems, obviously, to have more difficulty than a normal crow would, as he can't grip a branch with both feet. He has to more or less balance, or lean on, the clubfoot on the branch next to his good foot. Whenever he lands anywhere—on a branch, in a tree, or on the ground—he has to get himself adjusted before he can do anything or proceed anywhere. Everything is more difficult for him—everything. He reminds me of Jimmy Washington, the legless guy on the rolling cart who used to hang around at the corner of Kinsman and 59th. Remember him? And, of course, he reminds me of Broken Wing. I welcome his presence. I'm glad he is here.

I've been putting sunflower seeds and cracked corn out for him, especially. It's almost as if the ghost of Broken Wing has returned in the form of this crippled, deformed, club-footed crow. I'm fond of him. I hope he stays around. I haven't seen him for a day or two, though. I hope he's not gone off somewhere or been killed. I call him Lord Byron. What better name for a crow with a clubfoot?

With Lord Byron, as with Broken Wing, I've got a brother here with me, a deformed, tenacious, gritty, stubborn, obstinate, resolute black brother. May Lord Byron fight; may he resist; may he rebel; may he revolt until the last bitter—or not so bitter—moment of his life!

I wonder for Lord Byron, as I wondered for Broken Wing, whether he ever gets discouraged, ever wants to give up, give in, just die, because it's so much easier than to continue struggling. Think how much harder it is for Lord Byron, with that clubfoot, just to walk across the yard, just to get through each day.

Or maybe, on the other hand, when the struggle is the hardest, maybe that's when our instincts, or our will to live, or whatever you want to call it, drives us onward ever more strongly.

Whatever it is, what is certain is that this life is a struggle. Need I tell you? And those who don't know it, don't know even half of what it is to be alive.

Which reminds me of something else. I met a woman I know at the store the other day, and we were visiting, and somehow I got talking about the blues, and she said, "Well, what if you never get the blues?"

Can you imagine? I was speechless.

And she was serious, too. I must have had a look of incredulity on my face, because she looked at me and said, "No, really; what if you never do?"

I just shook my head. I wanted to say something, of course. I wanted to say to her, "If you didn't get the blues, honey, you'd be dead! You may be walkin' round, doin' your job, sweetheart, but you'd be dead."

But I didn't say it. I just smiled and changed the subject, because I figured I was talking to a corpse.

Sing 'em awhile, brother, make you feel a whole lot better.

Which is what White Throat and Lord Byron reminded me of. It's what I've been doing lately, and I'm feeling a little better, too.

And speaking of indigo moods, I've had an indigo bunting coming to eat the seed heads off the tall grass that grows just beyond the lawn, right here near the porch, every afternoon for about a week. It's rare in these parts to see these birds, so I feel especially fortunate. Always late in the afternoon. What a sight they are.

Your friend,

He finished the letter, put it in its envelope, sealed it, and then set aside the letter and the writing board. Yes, he was feeling better; a little better, at least.

The Man Who Lives Alone in the Mountains rocked and looked out at the summer afternoon, out past his garden and beyond to the mountains to the east, where the ravens lived and croaked and chortled their way through their lives. And he thought about all the other lives, both human and non-human, that come and go, come and go, come and go, here in this tiny little place, this slab of mountainside where he lived; and he smiled to himself, and knew he was a lucky so-and-so to be here and feeling so sad and blue, because he knew it was a sign that he was alive and still in love, with this life, and his life, and this world, and all the creatures therein.

11.

POSTLUDE

Then, like a bolt out of the blue, the blue of the sky, the blue of the indigo bunting, the blue of the blues, a little explosion went off inside The Man's brain, and he banged himself on the forehead with his open palm, as he was wont to do. He hadn't done that in a long time. A broad smile spread across his face, and he said out loud, "Okay. Okay."

The Man got up from his rocking chair on the porch, and went into the house and to his desk. He drew out from the desk drawer some more paper—a lot more paper. He grabbed a large handful of pencils and tossed them down on the desk, then sorted through them, chose a small handful he liked, and sharpened them; then took the paper and the pencils back outside to the porch, sat down in his rocker, put his writing board across the arms of the rocking chair again, and put the paper and the pencils on the writing board.

He stared out at the garden and the mountains beyond, but this time, he was not looking at them. Although it seemed he was looking outward, he was looking deeply inward, into that place inside himself from which the words come, that place his friend William called the Tone World—the source of all words and music. For a long time, The Man Who Lives Alone in the Mountains stared deeply into the Tone World. He listened closely. Then, again, a smile washed across his face. His pencil met the paper:

> Take the road going north,
> Further and further north.
> Go up through the valley,
> Between the mountain ranges
> Up to where the West Running River
> And the River Road go west. . . .

12.
A FINAL WORD

At the time of my arrival in this place, I knew nothing about The Man Who Lives Alone in the Mountains, and discovered nothing about him until my wife and I had built our own house here, and had been living in it for a number of years.

We came to where we are now forty years ago. When we first came to this place to build our own house among the ancient, pecker-fretted apple trees of this once and former side-hill orchard, I found the trees that The Man Who Lives Alone in the Mountains had cared for so diligently and carefully lying practically in ruin all around us, all of them choked with water shoots and crossing branches, dead trunks and limbs decaying in place and harboring insects and fungi of various kinds; making, of course, an ideal culture for more disease and decay. The whole orchard was, in short, entangled in the chaos of neglect.

After clearing land and building our house, I pruned the apple trees as best I could; but not being the orchardist The Man Who Lives Alone in the Mountains was, I lost many of the ancient trees to my own lack of knowledge of how to care for them; and among the trees I lost, I believe, there were numerous rare varieties of apples bred and developed over generations in this place by The Man Who Lives Alone in the Mountains and those who came before him here. How many unique species of apples did my own ignorance let slip back into oblivion? Ignorance and neglect may be passive cruelties, but they are cruelties nonetheless.

When a family, or a solitary individual such as The Man Who Lives Alone in the Mountains, first arrives in a place, builds a house, and tries to establish a life and puts down roots, there is little time for anything but the barest necessities of food, water, heat and shelter. It was therefore some time before I had even a little, more or less, free time to begin to get interested in the history of this place, and begin also to poke around among the rubble of old buildings lying about here to see what I could find.

There was—there still is—a cellar hole just below where we built our house which looked to me, since it was small, like the cellar hole of a house. The other clue that made me think this was the original house, and not some barn or outbuilding, was the ancient lilac bush still growing and blooming every May near the cellar. In these parts of the north, a lilac bush is a certain giveaway that this was once a dooryard, and that there will, therefore, be a cellar hole (or what was once a cellar hole) not far away. I surmised that this ancient and spreading lilac bush had been planted by a generation of settlers who'd come here long before the arrival of The Man Who Lives Alone in the Mountains. And, yes, there was indeed, not more than thirty feet from the lilac bush, a cellar hole, folding in upon itself, "closing like a dent in dough," as Robert Frost once said, choked with red raspberry bushes and a few half-mature poplar trees.

As I said, a few years after we had come here and settled into our lives here, one day, I began poking around down in the dingle-like declivity of that cellar hole. It was necessary for me to tear up raspberry bushes and chain-saw out of the way some of the poplar trees in order to get at what was beneath them. With a mattock and a pick, I began, more or less carefully, to paw at the decades of detritus turned back to soil that lay on top of whatever was beneath. I never imagined I'd become an amateur archeologist, but there I was, day after day, working my way down through years of history—toward what, I knew not.

The walls of the cellar had been laid up with fieldstone, put in place without mortar, but chinked with smaller stones, instead: a certain mark of the extreme age of this place.

First, I found some shards of charred timbers and some smoky broken glass, saying clearly that the demise of this dwelling came by fire.

I found also some broken pottery of no particular uniqueness, a kitchen fork, the upper ring of a galvanized pail, a rusted ax head, some equally rusted nuts and bolts, and the business end of a pair of lopping shears, the handles of which had long since rotted away. In other words, except for what was left of the lopping shears, the usual things one would expect to find in a ruin such as this.

Beneath those layers of the usual, however, as I dug deeper, I came upon, over in a corner of the cellar, in a kind of recess in the cellar wall, a most unusual discovery.

By removing a few of the fieldstones from the recess in the cellar wall, I was able to reach into a small open area actually outside the confines of the cellar and extract from this opening a strong steel box: not exactly a strongbox, but a strong box nonetheless. I was so excited by this find that I gave up my archeological dig and hurried with the box up the hill to my wood-shed/workshop, where I began carefully to chip away at the rust welding the hinges and the lid to the base of the box. With the addition of a little penetrating oil and patience, I was eventually able, slowly and gingerly, to lift the lid.

In the box, I found a package slightly larger than a ream of paper, say about three inches by 13 inches by 11 inches. The package was coated with wax. I surmised that the steel box and the waxed package within were able to survive the house fire because the box and its contents were actually outside the house and therefore insulated, to some degree, at least, from the intensity of the fire's heat.

I peeled away the wax to find the package covered with canvas and tied with a sturdy twine. I undid the twine, which was, in spite of its age, remarkably supple and well-preserved, as was the canvas wrapping. No doubt, the wax seal had preserved these.

Beneath the canvas and twine, I found yet another package, this one made of a whitish wrapping paper with a hard finish, the kind a butcher or fishmonger would use. This package was sealed, as well, with a strong fabric adhesive tape. I opened that package, also.

Inside it was an envelope—yet another package—and from it, I withdrew 183 neatly-typed manuscript pages, typed on a high-quality, high-rag-content bond. The first page said only:

BROKEN WING

No author's name appeared on that page, nor on any page of the manuscript.

As I read the story, I realized that it was the story of a life lived in this very place, the place where I live now.

The accuracy of the story amazed me. The ravens do, in fact, live in lofty aeries in the mountains to the east, and there really is a boreal bog above our house. The white spruce tree in which Broken Wing died is still there, below the lane near where the garden used to be, and now is again; and although the balsam fir from which White Throat sang is gone, the lilac bush, across the lane from where the balsam was, is still there, also. The details of what The Man Who Lives Alone in the Mountains had experienced in his place were so much like my own experiences, it seemed they could have actually been mine.

As I began to realize how this story I had found had taken place where I now live, I also began wondering about the person who wrote the story: this hazy, vague, mystery of a person known only as The Man Who Lives Alone in the Mountains.

First, I wondered, why would the so-called Man Who Lives Alone in the Mountains go to all the trouble to write this story down and type it up so neatly—all that, only to bury it in his own cellar? And if he were going to bury it, show it to no one, and literally hide it away, why would he go to such lengths to preserve it, to type it on a high-rag-content bond, which the author obviously knew would remain supple and not yellow for a long, long time, and to wrap it and wrap it again and again, and yet again, so thoroughly and carefully, and then put it in a steel box? If he wanted so badly to preserve this telling of his story, why didn't he publish it? What better way is there to preserve a story than to make many copies of it and pass them around?

The man himself was, and still is, a mystery to me. Shortly after I discovered this manuscript, I began asking old-timers around here if they had ever heard of this fellow, known only in this story as The Man Who Lives Alone in the Mountains. No one, not anyone, around here had any memory at all of such a man.

So I asked about the Bap Brothers, as they seemed to be a local reference outside the story itself. I was hoping the Bap Brothers might provide some locus, perhaps, to anchor the story; not only in this place, but hopefully in a specific time, as well. Again, no one anywhere around here had ever heard of a pair of brothers named Bap living on this part of the mountain. I looked in the phone book—I mean, in the current phone book—and there they were, a listing of about a dozen families with the last name of Bap; yet, no one around here remembers, or claims to remember, anyone by that name. All this seemed to me, at the very least, odd—and perhaps even suspicious.

And where did The Man Who Lives Alone in the Mountains come from? Was he from the north or the south? It's clear he came from a city, but which city? And where in the country was his uncle's farm?

What was this man, The Man Who Lives Alone in the Mountains, like? Where did he get his education? He was widely read, especially in, of all things, poetry. He knew the work of Ralph Waldo Emerson, Paul Laurence Dunbar, D H. Lawrence, Ikkyu, Hê Ching-chang, Mêng Hao-jan, Byron, and obviously many others he didn't mention in his story. In addition, and by his own admission, he was an orchardist and an ornithologist, as well. And, at one time, in another life, when he had lived in the city, a jazz musician, too. Who was this complex and interesting man, and why, in God's name, would he place himself on a remote and lonely mountainside in the middle of nowhere?

There was, it seemed to me, something of an answer to this last question, at least. At one point in the story, he says, in a letter to his friend Howard:

> What if I did come home? Who would know me? What good would it do? No. This exile is my home now, and it will always be.
>
> . . . I had to leave there, I had to leave home. I couldn't stand it there anymore. When I came here all those years ago, I was just trying to be who I am, and not who somebody else says I am—and that's what I'm still trying to be.

Although there is no sure way to prove my surmise, I think this passage and a lot of other things about the story indicate that The Man Who Lives Alone in the Mountains was African-American.

Neither I nor any other white person will ever know how difficult it is for an African American in this country to be who he or she takes a notion to be. They are defined on all sides by others. Whites constantly tell them who they are and must be in order to get on in the white world. And their own people also make demands upon, and assumptions about, who they are, how they should act, and what they should be interested in. Imagine how impossibly difficult it must have been for a man such as The Man Who Lives Alone in the Mountains to be who he wanted to be: a lover of books and poetry, of the wilderness and the mountains, a gardener, orchardist, and amateur ornithologist.

Put it another way. Now, of course, everyone knows that back in the days when this story took place—whenever that was—when The Man Who Lives Alone in the Mountains was alive, there were many, many well-educated black people in America, yet because of the bigotry of white America and the insistence on the part of whites to see black Americans as only one kind of person—and hardly a person, at that—the deep scholarship and learning of black Americans was denied and rejected; which, in fact, it then occurred to me, might be the main reason why The Man Who Lives Alone in the Mountains took to the wilderness in the first place. Was he simply, as he says, *just trying to be who I am, and not who somebody else says I am?*

I know there is no means in his story to prove it, but if The Man Who Lives Alone in the Mountains were an African-American, that could explain the Bap Brothers' hatred for The Man, and also The Man's deep identification with Broken Wing—another black soul stranded in a white world.

There is another haunting and disturbing thing I wonder about, and that is how the fire started—how the house burnt down. I wonder if the story that is beyond, outside, and behind this story is the story of how the Bap Brothers did, in fact, finally—after how many years— wreak their hatred and revenge upon this complicated man who wanted only to be left alone to raise apples, grow a garden, and feed the birds. I wonder if the Bap Brothers were able to do to The Man Who Lives Alone in the Mountains what Arnold was never able to do to Broken Wing.

And I wonder if The Man Who Lives Alone in the Mountains could see this inevitability coming toward him, like a storm coming over the mountains, and I wonder if that is why he wrote this story, preserved it, and secreted it away in such a clandestine and secure manner.

If this speculation is accurate, why, then, have all the people in this place erased from their collective memory any knowledge of these events? What kind of careful rewriting of history, what kind of willful forgetfulness is this? Why did they forget? What does that kind of willful forgetfulness say about the people who forgot?

All of this, of course, is mere speculation that could go on forever, alas, to no avail; but it is an interesting and important speculation nonetheless, for the kinds of issues it raises about the nature of The Man Who Lives Alone in the Mountains and the people around him.

There is yet another, even more confusing and distressing little fact about this story that I need to lay out here, as well.

Although I am, as I said, no orchardist, I am, as The Man Who Lives Alone in the Mountains also was, a devoted gardener. It was not at all difficult to see where The Man Who Lives Alone in the Mountains had had his garden. I therefore determined, for the sake of historical continuity—and also because I knew The Man would have built up the soil in that location to a level of richness and fecundity the surrounding soil would not have—to put my garden where his had been.

The first spring after I discovered and read *Broken Wing*, as I tilled the garden, I remembered what the story had said about the location of Broken Wing's grave: *I dug a little grave out at a far corner of the garden, so he could be close to all those garden insects he went after so diligently in my dream…I used the stones to make a little stone cairn to cover over the earth-scar, and also to keep off the grave robbers like the skunks. I drove the little sign on its stick into the ground just behind the stone cairn.*

I stopped the tiller and began to search the two "far corners" of the garden for evidence of the grave. I knew better than to look for the stick and the sign, which the winter snows would have broken down and the passing years rotted long ago. But a pile of stones doesn't rot, and although they do sink back into the earth, that takes a long time. I've seen stone piles in the middle of the big woods around here that were once in the middle of a pasture or a field, hand-picked, stone by stone, by the early settlers; stone piles more than a hundred years old. They are covered with lichen and moss, but they are there and evident, nonetheless; and although I didn't know exactly when the story of Broken Wing took place, I knew full well it wasn't anywhere near a hundred years ago. Therefore, I was certain that somewhere in the high grass, I would find a little pile of stones—Broken Wing's stone cairn.

I did not. Search as I might—and search I did, thoroughly, and again and again—I could find no evidence of any stone pile near the far corners of the garden. I knew that over the years, the frost heaves of winter would have scattered the stones of the cairn; but given all of these allowances, I still could not find even the slightest evidence of what was once a pile of stones. Again, I became suspicious.

Then, one June morning about six weeks after I'd put the garden in, something happened that not only surprised me, but also raised my suspicions even more.

I came out of the house early that June morning with my first mug of tea, bundled up against the June morning chill in my rubber barn boots against the heavy dew of the night, and headed out to the garden to look around. As I approached, I saw something scurrying up and down the newly-emerging rows of potato plants. I froze in my tracks. I could hardly believe my eyes. It was a rusty blackbird—no, two of them—moving about, pecking at some kind of bug on the surface of the garden soil. I backed away slowly, hoping not to disturb them, but they were more than aware of my presence, and as I began to move backward, they flew off.

The next morning, and many mornings that summer, instead of wandering out to the garden as the sun rose, I stayed in the house and watched the garden through my binoculars. On many mornings, I saw sometimes two, sometimes five rusty blackbirds, foraging around in the garden eating insects.

And since then, on many summer mornings, year after year, after my garden sprouts its crop of summer vegetables and the insects descend upon this new land of edibles, out of the high bog above the house comes a family of rusty blackbirds, who pick through the rows of vegetables, eating potato bugs and cabbage worms, slugs, and whatever other insects that day has to offer. They always seem to come in the early morning, and then again sometime in the middle of the afternoon.

Great confusion now joined my suspicions. There was no evidence of Broken Wing's grave, as the story said there should be; and there was, in fact, right out there in my garden right now, a family of rusty blackbirds, foraging for insects exactly as The Man Who Lives Alone in the Mountains said they did in his *dream*.

Confusion mounted on top of confusion.

In order to confirm or deny what The Man Who Lives Alone in the Mountains had said about the nature and habits of rusty blackbirds, I did a little research of my own, all of which only confirmed that hunting garden insects is definitely aberrant behavior for rusty blackbirds. They almost never venture very far from standing water, which is why they nest and breed in boreal bogs.

But here they were, right in front of me, almost every summer day: this odd little sub-species of rusty blackbirds which somehow, over generations, I suppose, has acquired a taste for potato beetles, cabbage worms, slugs, and other common garden pests. How did this happen? How did this subspecies evolve? Was it that their ancestor, one rusty fellow named Broken Wing, led the way for his progeny in acquiring this taste for garden insects?

Which leads directly to the question: isn't the presence of these rusty blackbirds every sum-mer in my garden *proof* that Broken Wing really did not die, but that he lived? That he was not just a character inside a dream that The Man Who Lives Alone in the Mountains happened to have on a particular midwinter night, but a real bird who left a real inheritance among his offspring—this liking for garden insects?

This strange and aberrant behavior in this little group of birds had to begin with some certain individual, did it not? It had to begin with a new form of behavior, and why could it not have been Broken Wing himself who began this little bit of odd evolution—because of the kindness of The Man Who Lives Alone in the Mountains? And since this happens here in this singular place and no place else, as far as I know, does that not prove that all these generations later, the rusty blackbirds in my garden are the direct descendants of a single bird whose name was Broken Wing, the very one in the dream in this story, the dream the author says is not true, but only a dream?

Here, a stumbling block presented itself to me, if only briefly. What did the successive generations of the descendants of Broken Wing do to maintain their interest in eating garden insects during those many years when there was no garden in this place? How could the genetic memory of something Broken Wing had begun carry over, stay alive, over numerous generations, without being reinforced? The question stumped me for a little while. Then I realized that although most birds like to return to the exact same place every summer to breed, and therefore the descendants of Broken Wing would very likely still be up above the house in the boreal bog, breeding generation after generation, they could very well have foraged further and further afield to find the garden insects they had gotten used to, in order to supplement the diet of insects they found in the bogs of their nesting sites. Thus, in this way, genetic memory could be sustained. And then when my garden had appeared, they—like all animals, and humans, too, for that matter—being creatures of opportunity, they just naturally seized upon the easiest path to what they needed and wanted, and as a matter of opportunity and convenience, returned to the garden closest to home once that garden had "returned" to their neighborhood.

With that minor conundrum solved, I returned to the deeper and more disturbing questions about this whole matter.

All the evidence seemed to be saying that a particular rusty blackbird named Broken Wing did exist—and did not die in a terrible winter storm, but lived on for a number of years and created a whole little subspecies of rusty blackbirds who added garden insects to their diet. They did all this, it seems, because of Broken Wing; and Broken Wing did it out of some kind of expression of interspecies trust between a rusty blackbird and a human being who called himself The Man Who Lives Alone in the Mountains.

All of this leads to a question: if what The Man Who Lives Alone in the Mountains wrote as fiction, as a dream, was actually a true story, if there actually was a rusty blackbird who did not die in that terrible winter storm, but survived as he did in the so-called dream—then why would The Man Who Lives Alone in the Mountains say it wasn't true, when in fact, it was?

Was The Man trying to hide something, or protect something or someone? Why did he lie? What and where are the answers to these questions?

Gradually, it seemed to me that going down the road of trying to find out why The Man Who Lives Alone in the Mountains had lied about the truth of the story was the wrong path to take. I began to wonder instead about the passage just after The Man wakes from his dream:

Now, The Man Who Lives Alone in the Mountains realized that the time from when he had gone to bed last night, through the spring and summer—the summer life of Broken Wing and his family—through the following fall, through the next winter and spring, and into the next summer, to the moment when that rusty blackbird had landed on the porch railing that August afternoon eighteen months from the time he'd gone to sleep—all of it, all of it all had been a dream.

How could it be a dream? It seemed so real! Had he not seen Broken Wing and his family hunting insects in the garden? Had he not seen Broken Wing perched on the top of his hoe handle? Had not Broken Wing come that summer afternoon and landed on the porch railing—stopped by for a little visit? Had not he seen spring, summer, and fall all come and go? And winter and the next spring, also? Had he not just seen that rusty black-bird on that August afternoon land on the porch railing and stare at him? How could all that be only a dream?

Yet outside the window right now, it was obviously not August. It was the morning after a terrible late-winter storm. Yes, that terrible storm. Yes, look, just look outside, all of it had to be only a dream. Yet, The Man Who Lives Alone in the Mountains won-dered to himself, how could he know that this, too, this moment right now, wasn't also just a dream? When are we awake? When are we dreaming? How can we tell one from the other? His dream had seemed at least as real as his waking! How can we tell one from the other? Right now: am I awake, or am I dreaming?

These questions seemed to me now to be the crux of the matter.

More and more, I began to see The Man's story as a kind of riddle, a *koan*, deliberately laid out in such a way as to not be unknotted by just anyone. What is dream, and what is not?

How do we sort truth from fiction, dream from waking? Is it necessary that we do so?

What if there is something—a land, say, a place beyond the conundrum, the mystery, to which we can go only when we accept the mystery and its confusions for what they are, and do not try to solve them? Perhaps, in that acceptance, we can gain a passport, so to speak, to that place beyond, that place The Man's friend William calls the Tone World…which, I believe, is where all stories come from.

And perhaps once we are able, through this acceptance, to go there, and once we have the skills to retrieve the story, once we are able to carry the story from the Tone World over to here, once we are able to do all that; perhaps then, the dualities of truth and fiction, of waking and dreaming, no longer matter, since now the story is here with us and part of us.

This line of reasoning, if you want to call it reasoning, led me to wondering about myself. If it weren't for the way I discovered this manuscript, if I hadn't actually found it in that box in the cellar, I could imagine that I had written this story. Put it another way: what if the story The Man Who Lives Alone in the Mountains wrote—the one called *Broken Wing*—what if that was a dream of *mine*?

If this whole story were *my* dream; if I dreamed there was a person like The Man Who Lives Alone in the Mountains, and he wrote a story about a bird with a broken wing, and in that story, The Man had a long dream in which the bird died—but in fact, he didn't die, because it was only in his dream, which was inside my dream—then that would explain why there were rusty blackbirds still in my garden, and it would also explain why the neighbors around here had never heard of The Man Who Lives Alone in the Mountains or the Bap Brothers. The neighbors around here hadn't heard of any of that because it was all in my dream.

And if Broken Wing *is* my dream, then it is also true that the story I have just told you about how I discovered the manuscript in the wall of that deserted cellar is a dream, as well. In other words, I dreamed I found a manuscript in a cellar wall called *Broken Wing*, and within the dream of how Broken Wing died was another dream, of how he lived—a dream of a dream in which there is a dream.

So, perhaps, here at the end, it may be, in fact, that I, after all, did write this story…although it surely doesn't seem that way to me.

THE END